Hope in New York City

THE CONTINUING STORY OF
THE IRISH DRESSER

Hope!

Cynthia Neale

By
Cynthia G. Neale

W̄M̄ WHITE MANE KIDS
KIDS SHIPPENSBURG, PENNSYLVANIA

Copyright © 2007 by Cynthia G. Neale

ALL RIGHTS RESERVED—No part of this book may be reproduced in any form without permission in writing from the publisher, except by a reviewer who wishes to quote brief passages in connection with a review.

This book is a work of historical fiction. Names, characters, places, and incidents are products of the author's imagination and are based on actual events.

The acid-free paper used in this book meets the guidelines for permanence and durability of the Committee on Production Guidelines for Book Longevity of the Council on Library Resources.

For a complete list of available publications
please write
White Mane Kids
Division of White Mane Publishing Company, Inc.
P.O. Box 708
Shippensburg, PA 17257-0708 USA

Library of Congress Cataloging-in-Publication Data

Neale, Cynthia G., 1954–
    Hope in New York City : the continuing story of the Irish dresser / by Cynthia G. Neale.
        p. cm.
    Summary: In New York City in 1849, fourteen-year-old Nora and her family struggle to make a living while dealing with rampant prejudice against Irish Catholics, and while her Da dreams of finding gold in California, Nora only wants to return to Ireland, despite catching glimpses of a better New York.
    Includes bibliographical references.
    ISBN-13: 978-1-57249-387-2 (pbk. : alk. paper)
    ISBN-10: 1-57249-387-9 (pbk. : alk. paper)
    [1. Irish Americans--Fiction. 2. Immigrants--Fiction. 3. Prejudices--Fiction. 4. Family life--New York (State)--New York--Fiction. 5. New York (N.Y.)--History--1775–1865--Fiction.] I. Title.
    PZ7.N2546Hop 2007
    [Fic]--dc22
                                                                2007002682

PRINTED IN THE UNITED STATES OF AMERICA

DEDICATED TO TIM NEALE,
MY WISE AND PATIENT FIRST READER.

CONTENTS

Chapters

Educational Resources

Chapter One

NORA'S EARLY MORNING ESCAPE

> To live, to err, to fall, to triumph, to recreate life
> out of life! On and on and on and on!
> —James Joyce, *Portrait of the*
> *Artist as a Young Man*

"Nora McCabe!" my sister, Meg, angrily whispers. She closes the door to the tenement building and boldly places herself in front of me so I am unable to leave.

She spits her words into my face, "Why are you dressed like a boy?"

I wipe my face with the back of my hand and stare out the window behind her head. I refuse to answer her because she will only lecture me as if she is a grand elder of our family.

"And why are ye wearing a boy's cap, a silly, dirty boy's cap?" she continues. I sigh, and stand as if in prayer, clasping my hands behind my back. I lift my chin high to where it points towards her mouth that never stops moving. I'm not listening!

I look out the filthy window of this tenement building we've lived in since coming to America from Ireland. The building is called a double-decker because it is two frame houses forced together side by side like two trees in a forest whose roots intertwine as one. Most of us living here are immigrants who shared the

1

same soil in Ireland at one time. We had been painfully uprooted when the potatoes rotted during the terrible Famine and we were forced to starve or leave the country. These roots that were once very deep in Ireland feel as fragile as this building we're crammed together in. And this new soil we share in America isn't full of good things to keep us rooted like the trees in a forest. It is plain old dirt and it covers us all the time.

The fancy dresses, colorful ribbons, and luscious cream cakes I once dreamed of are not a part of my new life in America. My family and I live one story up from the cellar in this putrid building. I imagine it being just one floor above the grave as I often see dead bodies being brought up by the health inspector and his workers. I told Meg it must be like hell down there and the dead people being brought up had to be going to heaven. She had a good laugh over my comment and said that the poor creatures would have to journey through Potter's Field to be buried before they'd ever get to heaven. Potter's Field is a shameful graveyard for the poorest immigrants and criminals, as if criminals and hungry people are equal in the eyes of God. Where are the eyes of God when all of these things happen?

I don't want to think of dead bodies or graveyards. I want to live and be amongst the living, but the terrible stench of rotten food, dead animal flesh, and sewage makes me feel like I'm amongst the dying. Mam says I should be grateful that we don't have the stench of rotting potatoes, but I'd prefer smelling rotten spuds to what I inhale every day in New York City. There's no milk and honey flowing on these American streets!

I long to dance in Ireland and lie in the morning's diamond dew drops to make myself beautiful, as the old widows used to tell us to do. I've never had enough times in the dew to make myself even slightly pretty. I was born with plain, brown, unruly hair and bright ginger freckles that are plastered all over my face. My Meg has beautiful red hair and creamy skin with just a few light freckles. She is altogether too lovely, but only in her face and not inside of her. She is eighteen and has ripened as pretty as a peach, but she doesn't understand the saying "pretty is as pretty does." I am very annoyed with her while she stands with her arms crossed and her tongue wagging at me.

"Dang you, Meg! You're ruining my plans!" I hiss at her, hoisting myself up on my toes to peer into her haughty face.

"Don't you be using Yankee cuss words on me, Nora McCabe!" she hisses back. "I know you've been running through the streets like a little guttersnipe!"

I turn away from her, but she grabs my shoulder, "It's nearly time for Da and Mam to wake and they'll be sick with worry if you're not home. You're going to go back into the kitchen and sit quietly while I make some tea. Then you're going to tell me why ye are dressed like a boy in the wee hours of the morning!"

I don't want to cause Mam and Da worry and so I walk back into the apartment and sit at the kitchen table. I'm afraid they'll awake to find me in boys' clothing, but I'm still planning on escaping Meg this morning. For now, I put my head down on the table and close my eyes. I usually leave at 4:00 a.m. and return by 8:00 a.m. to get ready for school. Mam, Da, and Meg leave by 6:00 a.m. to go to their work places and they think I'm still sleeping because I arrange my blankets and clothing on the floor next to the dresser to resemble my form.

I turn my head sideways and open my eyes to look at the dresser sitting in the corner of the living room. My dresser is an enchanted hiding place filled with stories and fairy dust. The inside of the cupboard is polished smooth with my tears because it was there that I encountered the angel of death and was given life. The fairies stitched up my broken heart many times although I have never seen them. I have felt them and know that God sends them to give me hope. And now I live in a New York slum where our Irish misery is a plague and heartache. For this reason, I love to lie on the floor next to the lower part of the dresser and look inside to remember, to dream, and to pray. I suppose I am too old to be crawling in the dresser these days, but it is still my place of hope.

The year is 1849 and it was over a year ago that my family and I left Ireland to sail to America. I sailed on a ship called the *Star,* and my family hid me inside the dresser because there wasn't enough money to purchase a ticket. At the beginning of the journey, I became separated from them and had to travel alone on the ship. I was frightened and filled with sorrow because I saw as much death on the ship as I had seen in Ireland. I became friends with Jack, a boy my age, but he died from typhus and the sea became his grave before our journey was over. My sister, Kate, also died from typhus and went to the sea grave when she traveled with my family on another ship. I've lived through a harrowing adventure and feel strong because of it, but I'm also looking around the corner wondering if more suffering is coming my way. Mam said that when I began my journey across the sea I was like a flower bulb that hadn't broken through the soil to meet the sun. She said that the darkness of the earth is important for a bulb to grow and the darkness in the hold of the ship was important for my growing, too.

"You've emerged with a large soul, my Nora, and ye are like the vibrant red fuchsia that grows wild in Ireland. You just need a wee bit of trimming so you don't grow too wild," Mam said in her stern mother's voice.

Leave it to Mam to describe it in lovely words, but sometimes living in America seems worse than our struggles in Ireland. I want to go home to Ireland, but while I am here, I will try to find my own American dream.

I consider climbing back into my blankets next to the dresser while Meg makes the tea, but soon my eyes close and I'm drifting to sleep until she shakes my shoulders.

"Tell me now where you're going dressed like ye are," she continues to whisper so as not wake our parents.

"I was just going for a bit of fresh air," I lie.

"Come now, Nora, there's no fresh air in this city. You'll have to be returning to Ireland for it," she says with a smirk.

"And to the fresh scent of rotting spuds?" I ask.

Meg places the teapot and cups on the table and sits down and pours our tea while glaring at me. She knows that if she is patient and stares at me long enough, I will probably give in and tell her the truth about where I'm going this morning. It's very hard for me to keep a secret, especially from my family.

Meg has become miserable and angry since arriving in America. We are all disappointed, but I won't be like her and cry in my soup, even if it is potato soup. Maybe there were no potatoes in Ireland, but we are able to buy them here. I think the very parts of my body are made with potatoes! I avoid Meg's eyes and look around the apartment while trying to keep my anger under control. I should be proud of my sister for finding work as a carder in a cotton factory. She works until 7:00 p.m. every day except Sunday and I'm hoping she'll marry one of the rich supervisors she works for, but she says they're all dirty pigs who only want one thing. I don't know what the one thing is, but it must be something wicked the way Meg said, "the one thing."

She takes a sip of tea and holds the delicate china cup in both hands. "Go on, then. Loosen your tongue!" she commands.

I take a gulp of tea and stare into the cup. I don't have to tell Meg anything, for she is not the boss of me!

"If ye don't tell me, I'll wake Mam and Da. They'll see you sittin' there all smug in a boy's vest, knickers, and cap. They'll think you've gone mad," she whispers hoarsely, leaning over the table.

"I'm a newsie, a real newsie! I sell newspapers for the *Sun* every morning! I've got meself a real job!" I blurt out, standing up. My tea cup tips on the saucer and tea spills onto the table. Meg is up in a flash to clean the mess, ignoring what I have just told her. I stand close to her while she wipes the table to tell her about my job and why I'm doing it.

"I meet my friend, Sean, at Printing House Square to buy the early morning newspapers to sell. He's from Ireland, too. You know we barely have enough money to pay the rent and there's never very much money left over for food or anything else. Don't ye want to have some ribbons for your hair, Meg?"

I tug on her shawl to try and make her look at me. "Don't ye want to eat something more than spuds and the wee bit of meat we scrape off the soup bones like dogs?"

Meg stops wiping up the table with a rag and throws it down onto the floor. She grabs my arm so tightly that I wince in pain. She doesn't realize she is squeezing a bruise that I received in my scramble to purchase newspapers the day before.

"I'll not have another sister, the only child left in the McCabe home, doin' herself in on the streets of this wicked city!"

"I made it alone across the sea, Meg! Nothing could be worse than the sea tossin' and turnin' me and making me ill near to death!" I pull away from her grasp and walk towards the door.

"Watch and see what I can do for myself and for all of us!" I say as I walk out the door. Meg follows and shuts the door behind us. The hallway stinks of alcohol, tobacco, and grease. Babies are crying and there are moans coming from someone sick.

"Please, Meg, let me go before Da and Mam wake up. I'm late! I'm late for the papers!"

Meg's mouth is curved downward and I don't wait for her reply. I push open the heavy outside door and run down the steps to the street and turn and wave as she stands in the doorway with her ugly frown. She opens the door and yells, "Holy Joseph! My wee sister, the newsboy, is sellin' the papers right off the presses!"

As I hurry to meet Sean, I envision Meg tiptoeing back into the apartment and boiling more water for tea. She'll be drinking tea and eating a piece of soda bread, reminiscing about our life in Ireland and how we daydreamed about America. We thought our lives here would be full of tortoise shell combs, ribbons for our hair, and comfortable feather beds to sleep in, and, of course, never having to experience hunger pangs again. I shudder in the dampness of the morning, but also because I remember the Famine dead being dumped into mass graves as we traveled on a neighbor's cart to get to the port to leave for America.

I can hear Meg say as she looks around the apartment, "How silly of us McCabes! A pigsty in Ireland would be better than this place!" She repeats this every day. Once she told Mam and Da that we should sell my dresser and purchase comfortable beds and bedding. I nearly punched my sister in her face for suggesting such a thing.

"I can never live without my dresser," I say aloud, wrapping my arms around my waist to try and keep warm. "It'll always be my special place even if I can't fit inside!" My sister Kate understood my feelings I have for my dresser. Sadness suddenly slips into my steps when I think of Kate now buried in the Atlantic Ocean.

"My dresser . . . I love to say 'my dresser'!" I look around to see if anyone has heard me, but I'm quite alone as I walk. Sometimes I like to pretend I'm hovering in the air above my life and then I can gain a better view of it. I can appreciate it because I can see it so much better when I am looking down upon it. I do this as I walk, and in my mind's eye as I float above New York, I see my dresser as it fits into the corner of the living room in our cramped apartment. We live in Five Points, a neighborhood that is a brutal and wretched part of New York City. Our tenement has no running water except from one dirty tap in the hallway that is used by everyone. There are plenty of little running bugs, however. Death still surrounds the Irish people, but it isn't the British starving us this time. It is America starving us of our dignity, and the Irish are killing each other and anyone else who gets in their way. Perhaps it takes only a few days for an Irishman full of foolish dreams to become a depraved American. I wonder if I will become one, too.

"What is left in Ireland?" I say aloud, kicking up the dust in the road, trying to still hover in my imagination. "Are there only bits and pieces left?" Our cousin has sent one letter since we came to America and it was full of news of death and empty cottages.

Maybe we have a little more to eat here, unlike what we'd have if we were still in Ireland, but there is emptiness in our lives now. I remember more than the death angel visiting our hungry land. I haven't forgotten the flowering glens, sea-washed towns, and open fields that are nowhere in my life now. Here in America we live on garbage-strewn, muddy, and cobbled streets where there are rows of tenement buildings shutting out the sky's vast light.

I reach into my pocket for the coins I have saved. I drop them into my boot for safekeeping. I'll be buying the newspapers with them this morning. "There's nothing like a bit of money in a girl's boot to put a smile on her face," I say proudly as I run down the street to meet Sean.

Chapter Two

LOOK AT ME NOW IN AMERICA!

Slow bleak awakening from the morning dream
Brings me in contact with the sudden day.
I am alive this I.
—Harold Monroe, "Living"

I stop running and creep, catlike, through the narrow streets in the early dawn to get to the newspaper office. I have watched my cat, Paws, tiptoe soundlessly to a mouse and snatch it in her mouth. I never had a cat like Paws when we lived in Ireland. I did have Miss Maggie Hen and Mr. James Pig, although they were not supposed to be my special pets. Our animals in Ireland had to be sold in the market, except Da had a soft heart and allowed me to keep Miss Maggie and Mr. James until we were forced to sell them when the Famine came. Here I am in America with a cat as vicious as a tiger if she wants to be, and she is teaching me how to survive in this strange city.

I shiver in the cold spring morning air. Soon, I'll be selling papers dressed as a newsboy on the streets of New York! I move as stealthily as Paws and make my way to Printing House Square. I pretend to have cat's eyes, too, but I don't see the dead horse lying on the side of the street and stumble onto it. The poor thing only smells a little as I fall on its hard and bloated belly. I struggle to get back on my feet and wonder what happened to this horse and how it came to be here. No matter, for this is New York and I often see dead animals lying on the street. This is life in America. No magic cows, just dead horses, and men and boys who club dogs and each other to death. I have learned how to maneuver these dirty streets in the wee hours of the morning, but this is the first time I have fallen on a dead horse. I walk away as quickly as I can, for I can't be worrying about another dead animal in the street. I feel cold and when I touch my face, it is wet from the dampness of the morning.

"The dew drops of the fairies have nowhere lovely to light," I say. "There are no tiny flowers here for their mornin' visit."

Out of the gray morning light that is tinged with the colors of a new day, comes a surprise. Sean is alongside me dressed in an oversized, tattered, checkered cap, green plaid knickers, and a dirty white shirt. He is wearing old boots without their laces that are much too large for his feet. He is a bony, red-headed, freckle-faced Irish lad of fifteen years.

"Your face 'tis the flower for the fairies to light upon, Nora. The only flower from Ireland I know!" His face reddens for being so forward. I can't believe my ears, and before there is any further awkwardness, he yells, "Let's race!"

We run through the streets scattered with pink sunshine beginning to pour forth from the heavens; there are early morning newsboys and peddlers with their pushcarts preparing for a long day. Sean wins the race and as I come up behind him, he turns and says, "Tuck your hair away! They might see you're a girl and you won't get your share of papers!"

"Are we too late?" I ask, quickly pushing my thick mop of knotted hair underneath my cap.

"There'll be plenty of papers. Do you have enough money?" Sean asks. Once I had only enough money to purchase five papers and he tried to buy me more, but I wouldn't think of it.

"I've coins in me boot, and it's killin' me to walk!" I say as I stomp my foot.

The newsboys lining up in front of the newspaper office called the *Sun* believe I'm a frail boy just off the boat from Ireland. I'm proud to be a part of this enterprise, although it is made up of only boys. We use our own money to purchase the dailies or the penny papers to sell. We also take a loss for whatever papers we don't sell. Most of the newsboys live on the streets or in a special lodging house and pay a few cents a night for a bed in a dormitory. They also pay a few cents more for bread and coffee for breakfast, and pork and beans for dinner. I'd like to move into the lodging house if I could pull off being a boy. My mouth waters every time Sean describes the food they eat.

We aren't the only children selling something on the streets of New York. There are children, as young as six or seven, selling matches, flowers, shoelaces, and ribbons. There are German, Irish, and Italian children uttering their own languages and scrapping with one another to compete for the best customers. It's always noisy and boisterous on the streets, and I miss the birdsong of Ireland. Most of the children are newcomers to America. I think hope must ride high in our childish hearts because we are the peddlers of the impossible on these wretched streets of New York. I survived the ship fever coming over to this country and I know I can survive living here, too. Sometimes I imagine traveling first class back to Ireland on a clean passenger ship. It will be a different Ireland, an Ireland with lots of food for all of us like we used to have at our Cake parties. At our Cake parties, everyone would bring something to raffle off to raise money for a struggling family. There would be music, dancing, and plenty of food. When I return to Ireland, I'll live in a big house like the landlord or his agent lived in. All the landlords and agents will have packed up and moved away forever! I wonder if this is a wasteful dream, but anything is possible. Look at me now in America! Who would ever have thought I'd be a newsie selling papers on the streets of New York.

Here in New York, the Irish stick with Irish, the German stick with German, and so forth. There are some of us who speak only Irish, but most of us speak English. It doesn't matter if we speak proper English, as long as we can communicate what it is we're selling.

"Try to be quiet," Sean says as we come closer to the *Sun*. "Some of them newsies are sleeping, and if we don't wake them, we'll be sure to get more papers." Sean came from Ireland a few months before I did. He lost a sister to the ship fever on his journey, but he doesn't like to talk about it the way I like to talk about my own experience coming over here. We met a couple of weeks ago in front of the *Sun*. He tried to push me aside to buy more papers, but after I bought my share, we became friends.

Four disheveled boys are sprawled out and sleeping on the pavement in front of the *Sun*'s doors when we arrive. One boy stands to his feet and nudges the others with his foot to wake them. Soon, all four dirty and tattered boys are yawning and cursing in front of the office. Two of the boys speak a strange language, but I recognize cursing in any language.

I shake my foot to count the coins with my big toe to see if I have enough to buy an armload of papers. If I sell all the papers, I'll have money to buy special bread and new shoelaces for Meg's and Mam's shoes. I'll also need to save some of my earnings to purchase tomorrow's papers.

One of the boys kicks at the gate. "Open up!" he yells.

He is as thin as a pencil and must live on the streets and not in the lodging house run by the Society of Poor Children where there is pork and beans served every day. My mouth waters as I've only eaten stale soda bread. I am sometimes still hungry in America, but I've never been as hungry as I was in Ireland.

The boy punches the newsboy next to him and accuses him of stealing his money. Where would these boys get their money to buy papers in the first place? Da told us about the boys who club old women to steal their money when they walk to the market. I am frightened to think these boys could be real gangsters.

I whistle with my hands in my pockets as I walk closer to Sean, trying to act like a boy. I motion for him to move to the other side of the street. I need to feel safe until the doors open.

"Do you have enough cash?" I ask him after we walk away from the other boys.

He nods and smiles. "How did you ever get enough money to buy your first bundle of papers?"

"Girl's work; nothing but good ole girl's work," I say quietly, "and not from selling matches, songs, and flowers, either. I helped my Mam with the laundry and ironing she does for a rich family. She gave me some of her earnings and told me to save it in my dresser, but when I saw there was only enough money to pay for our rooms and to send a little money back home to Ireland, I knew something had to be done. There's more than bread and spuds for us to eat here in America. The butcher sells more meat than we've ever seen in our lives, but there's never enough money to purchase the good cuts. The bones are what we buy! Nothing but bones, like we're dogs!" I'm angry and clutch the sides of my pants, nearly pulling them down as I speak.

Sean is embarrassed by my outburst and turns away to look at the boys arguing in front of the *Sun*.

What would he know about soup bones when he has pork and beans to fill his belly!

"Girls like me have to be innovative to make money in America. When Meg and I saw the boys selling newspapers in front of City Hall, I knew I could do it, too. There were flocks of people herding to their offices and on their way they snatched up newspapers and threw coins at the boys. The sun was shining directly on those coins and they looked like big pieces of gold. I thought that this was why we heard America had streets paved with gold. I decided right then and there that I would turn myself into a boy so I could have some of America's gold, too. I listened to the newsies crying out their slogans that day:

"'Ere's your *'Erald*!"

"Mornin' *Times*!"

"Buy a *Tribune*!"

"'Nuther Murder!"

"Orful shootin' scrape!"

"'Orrible accident!"

I say these selling slogans in a boy's deep voice and Sean smiles at me. I'm proud of myself for getting just the right accent for each one.

"Ye're doing a fine job in the sellin' business," Sean says. I blush and turn to look at the boys crowding around the *Sun*. One yells for the doors to open, and then the rest join him. They sound just like morning roosters crowing noisily for the *Sun* to open its doors!

"Maybe someday I'll sell oysters. They're as popular as the papers."

"You, Nora, wouldn't be suited as a fishmonger. I can't see you blowing the fish horn," Sean says.

I laugh because I can picture the old smelly fish woman blowing a loud horn and calling out, "Fresh Fish Here . . . Going Fast." She better sell it fast or she'll be calling out, "Fresh Fish Here . . . Going Bad!"

"What do you think about me selling fruits and berries?" I ask. "Then I can shout out, 'Raaaaspberrrries!

Blaaaaaaackberrrrrrries!' And after selling the berries, I can hawk wood and cry out, 'Wud! Wud! Wud! Wud!'"

I laugh so hard that I have to sit down on the street. My cap comes off and my hair falls down my back.

One of the boys in front of the *Sun* points at me and yells, "He's a girl! A stupid girl trying to take our papers!"

Another boy shouts, "She's not honey-fuggling us. I knew he was a girl all along. Let's hope she's earning money to go back to where she came from. Maybe she'll take some of her rabble with her."

I'm boiling mad and ready to pounce on the boys with my fists, but the gates to the *Sun* open and we scramble to pick up big bundles of the dailies that are being set out. A young boy, who appears to be only five or six, picks up a bundle and topples to the ground. He loses his grip on the papers and they fly around the street.

"You'll be paying for those papers, lad!" an employee of the *Sun* yells at the boy.

I forget about the bundles of papers I was going to buy and help the poor boy pick up his newspapers that are being eyed by other street vendors as they float around the street.

"Holy Mary and Joseph! Help him, Sean!" I yell.

Sean and I pick up the boy's papers, but in the meantime, the other boys buy most of the papers and there are just a few bundles left for us to purchase.

"I've enough money for three bundles," I say to Sean as I watch him buying all that is left.

I grab three bundles from him and kick off my boot to get my coins. The coins fall onto the street and my bootless foot has an awful odor that even Sean, who isn't that clean himself, notices. He wrinkles up his nose and turns away from me. I quickly put my boot back on and pick up my coins. I see Sean wink at the *Sun* employee as he takes his money for the rest of the papers. The man looks at both of us and chuckles.

"I've never seen the likes of you Irish—scrapping with each other one minute and helping each other the next."

My heart is pounding as hard in my brain as in my chest, so hard that I can barely think straight. Sean has taken all the papers! I can't even trust my own people in this city. I'm nearly in tears, and they don't come as easily as they used to.

"You saw it yourself, sir," I say to the man. "This boy took all the papers while I helped the young lad over there."

The employee laughs and goes back into the building.

Sean places three bundles of newspapers on the street in front of me.

"What do you mean by this, Sean O'Connolly!"

"There's no 'O' in me name, now," he says. "I lost the 'O' after I got off the ship. I'm buying the papers for you. I hoard me money, but you care for your family. You're a better person than I am."

"I'm not so good. Sometimes I buy the long cinnamon stick candy and eat it without anyone in my family knowing," I say to him, embarrassed by his charity and my lack of trust.

"Ahh, Nora, let a poor lad help you out," he says, "but next time I'll buy you a stick of the long-lasting candy."

"Don't you be pitying me, Sean O'Connolly."

"How could I pity a girl who has a heart of gold and a big cart of dreams to pull around for all her tomorrows?"

"Be off with us, then!" I say. "And thanks be to God for the papers as a token of your friendship." I pick up the bundles, feeling uncomfortable with his fancy remarks.

"Same time tomorrow," he says. "And don't forget your cart of dreams!" I notice his dirty teeth and that his freckled face is as red as his hair. Ginger-haired people can never hide their feelings. Mam and Meg give their hearts away, too, when their faces color the same as their hair.

I adjust the papers in my arms, feeling light-hearted although my load is heavy. Sean is really a good friend, I think, and for a moment I know that all is right in God's world, although this world is in America and not in Ireland.

Chapter Three

HELGA'S BAKERY

> Silence? What can New York—noisy, roaring,
> rumbling, tumbling, bustling, stormy, turbulent
> New York—have to do with silence?
> —Walt Whitman

Sean gave me good advice on how to sell lots of newspapers. Three bundles are much too heavy and cumbersome to carry around to sell and make change with customers.

"Ask Mr. Switzer if you can keep two bundles inside his grocery store while you sell one bundle," he instructed me. "Offer him a paper for his inconvenience. He'll shake his head and then place coins in your hand. He'll do this each time you go there."

"Every day?"

"A few days with Mr. Switzer and then do the same thing at Leona's Fruit Stall on Broad and Main. Take turns with each one, and not only will they not mind, you'll make a profit," Sean stated proudly.

I make my way along Broad Street after depositing two bundles with Mr. Switzer. I begin to cry out, "Murder, Murder! Read All About It!" and "News, News! Hurry for the News!" I pass by men staggering with heavy bundles of cloth. They are carrying unfinished pieces from factories to be sewn in their tenement apartments. Their homes are called sweatshops and

19

Da said we should have one, too. He doesn't like Mam going into a rich person's home to wait on them hand and foot. He says it's like being a servant in the landlord's big house in Ireland, but Mam won't have us sewing factory pieces in our home because the workers become ill from the dye in the cloth. Their white Irish skin becomes colored because they work day and night buried in the dyed cloth.

A few days ago, I went with Sean to the apartment his mother and father live in. They share it with other families and there's no room for him to stay there. He has to live at the lodging house like an orphan, but he says he likes it better than living with his father. The apartment is a sweatshop on the fourth floor where the smells of frying fish and onions attacked my hunger something fierce when we entered the front door of the building. Two men, three women, two young girls, and a boy sat sewing trousers and vests. It was a bit of a shock to see their faces, hands, and arms black from the dye, but there was a lot of energy in the room, desperate energy that was as strong as the wind in Ireland. It was the same energy I experience on the streets selling my papers. I stared at them and stumbled over the dozens of pants piled upon the floor. When I made apologies, no one paid me any mind. They didn't even notice I was there!

Before we left, I convinced Sean to give his money from selling the papers that morning to his mother. He placed the money on her lap and she looked up at him with tears in her eyes.

"Thank you, lad," she said.

Sean's father gave him a beating the next day when Sean stopped in at the sweatshop apartment. He told him to stay away from his Mam and concentrate on taking care of himself.

Sean told his Mam that he was saving money to buy the fare for both of them to go back to Ireland. He has many aunts, uncles, and cousins who would welcome them home, he said. I feel sorry for Sean, but he wants no pity from me. I can understand because I don't want any pity, either. Sean has some bruises on the outside of him that his father put there, but I can see the dark purple bruises on his insides. They're worse than what shows on his skin.

"News! Here's the News!" I yell as I walk down the street. I've been so engrossed in my thoughts that I don't see a couple of bootblacks lumbering down the street with their homemade shoeshine kits looking to polish some fancy shoes of the rich.

"Go on your way, Paddy!" one of them snarls as he kicks my leg. I quickly run away from him and tears fall without my control. I wipe them away as I rub my leg and clasp the papers underneath my arm. I shake my head back and forth and try to forget the things that have happened since arriving in America. Most of the children peddling their wares on the streets of New York are filled with hatred. Sometimes I feel I can't endure any further cruelty in this new country, but it's a new day, a new beginning, and the sun sure shines more here than in Ireland.

"New York Is Exploding with Promise! Read All About It!" I shout, holding up the newspaper. Honestly, "promise" is not a word in the headline, but using a positive word will bring more sales. The article is about the city exploding with people and how rapidly it's becoming dangerous.

Two hours pass and I sell all but my last paper from the remaining bundle. The coins are jingling in my pocket and I'm full of excitement. I'll hide my last paper in the dresser and surprise Da after his long day working at the bank where he cleans and runs messages for the clerks. I walk by a tenement alley and see a few boys playing stickball with a broom handle and rubber ball. Sean said that stickball is the game of immigrant boys. He also said that baseball is the most popular sport of the day and it's all right for a boy to not know how to read or write, as long as he has a detailed knowledge of baseball heroes and statistics. I stop to watch them play and after a few minutes, I hear barking behind me. I turn around and a big yellow dog with a rib cage nearly protruding out of its sides lurches at me. I fall to the street and the dog nuzzles my head. I am going to be eaten alive! The boys playing stickball come to my aid and beat the dog with the broom handle.

"Look!" one of them yells. "There's money everywhere!" My coins have spilled out of my pocket and the boys are picking them up off the street.

"Don't steal my money!" I stand up and try to retrieve my coins but they've already picked them up.

"You owe us the money for saving your life!" a boy says as he runs away in the direction the dog ran in. I hope the yellow dog mauls those darn boys!

Boys! They are as vicious as the dogs and pigs that roam the streets of New York. Anyone can be attacked by stray dogs if they have food in their hands or pockets. There are mad dogs sought after by gangs of boys who club them to death and bring in their carcasses to get paid fifty cents for each one. Those boys who have stolen my money are going after the dog that knocked me down. Then they'll have my money and fifty cents more.

"I hope that dog tears your face off!" I sit down on the street feeling defeated. "It's unfair! Life in Ireland was unfair and life in America is unfair!"

I rub the dirt off my clothing and leave black marks because my hands are stained with newsprint from the newspapers. My cap has fallen off again and my ugly hair tumbles down my back. I look over at the early morning peddlers who are setting up their pushcarts and selling their wares. They ignore my plight for this is an everyday occurrence for them. They are used to street gangs fighting and yelling their fever pitched ultimatums. The only person who takes notice of what happened is Mrs. Filippio who stares at me as she stands next to her pushcart laden with produce. She is wearing a worn-out red kerchief on her gray head, and draped over her shoulders is a crocheted black shawl full of big holes. She is short, stocky, and as mean as a bulldog, a wild one at that. She's known to never give in to a haggling customer, repeating, "You like, you buy. You don't like, you don't buy!" When a customer tries to obtain a lower price, she waves her arms and shouts in Italian. Then the customer will throw the money down and grab the purchase, eager to get away from her loud cursing. I always stay far away from Mrs. Filippio's stall! There are usually one or two pudgy, red-cheeked toddlers hiding in her skirts, their drool pouring out of their dirt-crusted mouths.

I smile weakly at Mrs. Filippio, my lips trembling with frustration. To my amazement, she marches over to me, pushing her children out from underneath her skirts. They follow her and watch wide-eyed as their mother approaches me. My mouth twitches but I still smile at her.

"You!" she shouts as she points a finger at me, "You go to school!" Before I realize what she is doing, she yanks me off the street and drags me over to her stall. Her children crowd around me and try to reach up to touch my hair. She picks out a large, shiny, red apple from her cart and shoves it into my hands.

"Take apple . . . no buy, no buy . . . Go to school!" Then she pushes me towards the street.

"Thanks be to God for you," I say, shocked by her behavior. It is more surprising to have someone treat me with kindness, for I am used to hostility and meanness.

I walk away thinking about the plight of this topsy-turvy world I live in. There is both evil and good, but today some of the good poked through the evil. I don't have any coins to buy bread or tomorrow's newspapers, but I have this good apple on an evil street where boys think they rule! I polish the apple on my shoulder where there is no newspaper print and talk to myself as I walk towards home. After a few minutes, I clutch my apple in one hand and the newspaper in the other and run as fast as I can down the street, dodging in and out of the crowds. I fly past the bakery, the fishmonger, and more produce stalls. Yeasty bread smells taunt my hunger and the smell of the sea on the fish nauseates me. I don't like fish because the scent of the ocean took up residence in my memory after I climbed out of my dresser when the *Star* landed in New York. I stop running and stand on a corner in a pool of sunlight that is flowing between two old buildings. I reach into my pockets and dig deeply to see if there are some coins left after the incident with the dog and boys. Grimy sweat trickles down my face and onto my arms as I search my pockets.

"Holy Mary, Mother of Jesus, please help me . . ."

I find a few coins and hold them up in the sunlight one by one. "Thanks be to God and His fairies!"

A parade of good and evil marches down these streets day and night and I must find my own steps to avoid the evil and get in line with the good. If only I knew how to avoid the evil! The coins feel smooth and hopeful in my hands, and I safely place them back into my pocket. I can now buy something for my family and still have enough money to buy a few newspapers to sell tomorrow! My stomach growls and I remember the lovely aroma coming from the bakery I ran past. I decide to walk back to the bakery to purchase some delicious bread for all of us. When I find the bakery, I open the heavy green door with the sign "Helga's Bakery" over it. I walk inside and the delicious smells intoxicate my senses and make me dizzy. I hear strong and orderly speech that must be the German language; these are familiar sounds I often hear on the streets of New York. It might be a real language, but it sounds like gibberish to my ears. My tenement building is filled with Irish people from places all over Ireland I have never heard of, and in the building next to ours there are a few German families living next to Irish families. We don't talk to the German people very much, nor do we invite them to tea. Mam said she would like to find out if they drink tea, but she thinks it is ale they like, and if it is, then the Irish and German people might have something powerful in common. We watch them from our windows and when we sit on our steps, but we only get close to them in the marketplace. They stand behind their pushcarts on the streets where people from around the world bargain for the best prices in their best tongues.

I am shaking when I walk into this world of heavenly sweets that only the fairies could have made in this city. I look around at the customers talking to one another and waiting in line at the counter. Many of them stop talking and stare at me. I turn away from their strange faces and peer into the display case where there are more sweets than I've ever seen in my life. This is the America I dreamed of! I don't know how I'll choose one sweet over another. I am nearly drooling as my eyes take in all the delicacies and I wipe my mouth with my hand and fear I have wiped more dirt onto my already dirty face. As I look at the breads and pastries, I think about the cornmeal America sent over to us when we were starving from the Famine. We became sick from it because of its strange flavor, and I wonder why America never sent us some of these delicious breads.

I place a coin on the counter because I want to purchase the long loaf of puffy twisted bread with icing and raisins. My eyes feast on the piles of doughy sugar-topped buns and loaves of rich dark bread. Bounty! It's here in America all right! I've seen plenty of food in the pushcarts and grocers; even smelling food I didn't want to smell, but this is more than we ever had at our Cake parties in Ireland! This must be why Mam said it was best we didn't go into the bakeries to be drooling over what we couldn't afford, and that her soda bread would have to suffice. This is the first time I've been in a bakery in America and I am nearly fainting with desire. Mam said Cork City in Ireland had a lovely bakery, but I had never gone there.

There are mostly women in the bakery and they look like Mrs. Filippio, except they are lighter in their skin and hair color. They must be wide from all the food they're blessed to eat every day of their lives from this bakery. I wait for the woman behind the counter to wait on me but she keeps walking past me and waiting on everyone else. I pick up the coin and place it back down again, trying to get her attention. I'm afraid to look at any one person, but out of the corner of my eye, I see someone pointing at me. I feel my face redden with anger and I don't know what to do. I listen to women speak to one another in their own language, but I hear a few English words and begin to understand what they are saying. I stand like a statue as I hear them say that they have never seen such a dirty boy with long matted hair like a girl's. It occurs to me that I must appear very silly dressed in boys' clothing with my long hair hanging out of my cap. My newspaper is becoming crumpled as I hold it underneath my sweaty arm. I'm in a hurry to buy the bread and leave this strange, but wonderful, bakery.

"Not enough!" the woman behind the counter huffs as she stops in front of the display where I am standing. Then she continues waiting on the other customers, pretending I'm not there.

"I've more coins to purchase the bread," I say, trying to ignore the tears heating up in the back of my eyes; they sting my brain as they stay stuck there. I place another coin on the counter. I wait a few more minutes, but I'm ignored.

I place the shiny red apple on the counter next to my coins. A low rumble of laughter fills the room and it feels like the sound of an earthquake that will swallow me whole. I wipe the tear that has forced itself out of my brain and wish that I had never come into this shop with the tantalizing aromas and unusual people.

"I can pay with this apple, too," I say, and there is more laughter.

"They're not like Irish people," I think, "who'd give a child their last piece of bread if they had it."

"A little guttersnipe!" someone utters in poor English. I feel my chest puff up with indignation, for I can speak better English. My pride rises within me like hot steam off the kettle, but I hold my tongue.

"A street orphan," another person whispers.

I stand at the counter stiff as cardboard. I want to shout that I am not an orphan or a guttersnipe, but I will declare my stubbornness by not moving until I'm waited on like any other paying customer. I am a newsie and deserve some respect! After a few long minutes, the woman behind the counter walks over to me and tugs at my cap. Then she opens the display window and picks up the luscious loaf of bread I'm hungering for and places it in my arms. She picks up Mrs. Filippio's apple, lays it on top of the bread, and then picks up the two coins and walks out from behind the counter. I stand embarrassed by her sudden kindness when she drops the coins into my right pocket.

"Go to school!" she says, smiling and revealing a missing tooth. I turn to leave and an old man wearing a similar cap to mine walks over to the door to hold it open for me. I feel warmth from the bread that must have just been taken out of the oven. I press it to my heart, this heart of mine that is both brave and fearful, and it is warmed as well. Now I have a special treat for my family, as well as hope in the people who live and work on these streets of New York that are not paved with gold. It is the digging for gold here I'll have to be doing, but I think this gold will be a different gold than I ever imagined.

Chapter Four

SCHOOL

From childhood's hour I have not been
As others were; I have not seen
As others saw: I could not bring
My passions from a common spring.
From the same source I have not taken
My sorrow; I could not awaken
My heart to joy at the same tone;
And all I loved, I loved alone.
                              —Edgar Allan Poe

Every adult I encountered on the streets this morning has shouted at me to go to school, and after the bakery episode, I hurried home to get ready. I will be late, but better late than never! I untangle my matted hair and wash it as best as I can. I long for Mam to braid my hair and tie it with a lovely ribbon, but she has gone to work and we don't own any ribbons. The wooden barrel of water setting in the kitchen has already been used by everyone in the family, and it is cold and dirty. I usually wash myself with a rag in the evenings, but washing away the filth of New York City requires more than a dab of water here and there.

Meg and I carry water into our apartment from the community faucet in the dark hallway on the first floor every morning and evening. People fight to get there first because the faucet is shared by ten or more families. Besides hauling a few buckets of water every day, we have to empty our chamber pot in the filthy outhouse in the back of the tenement building. Mam won't allow us to use the toilets in the outhouse because the landlord doesn't have the sewage carted away every week and sometimes it sits there for over a month. Meg and I take turns dumping the pot in the outhouse and we have to put a rag over our mouths and noses or else we'll get sick from the smell. We are the fortunate ones to be living in rooms facing the street and not the back where the outhouse is. Even if it is noisy, at least we do not have to smell the putrid odors coming from the sewage.

When we first arrived in America, we stayed with Aunt Bridget in her one-room apartment and were crammed together like pigeons in a cage, sleeping on the floor side by side. It isn't much better now, except that we have two rooms, a table, and four chairs. We also have my dresser and when Irish neighbors visit, jealousy shines in their eyes as they admire it. They remember Ireland and how their dressers sat next to the hearths in their cottages. There is no hearth here, only a smoky coal burning stove to boil a few bones with little meat on them for soup. When we first arrived, Aunt Bridget fed us lots of meat that made us ill because our starved bodies weren't used to the abundance. It is so different here than in Ireland, except for some of the hunger pains we experience occasionally because there isn't enough money to buy food to satisfy our appetites. There are berries in the market, but they aren't for me to pick freely like I did from the fields at home.

My clothes are tattered and dirty no matter how much I try to mend them and wash the city's filth out of them. I have a shift made out of burlap that I put an apron over when I'm not in school or wearing boys' clothes to sell the papers. I have another dress that

Aunt Bridget made for me to wear to school when we first moved here.

After getting ready for school, I rush through the busy streets, my heart beating in fear of the teacher who will lecture me for being late. I arrive and endure the reprimands, squeezing myself into my desk. I tower like a giant sunflower that hangs its head after a short bloom. And it isn't because I am too tall; I am rather short for my age. I'm humiliated to be a fourteen-year-old in a first grade classroom! I'm stuck in a class with little children who are babies compared to my age!

There is only one other child, an ugly boy who is fresh off the boat from Germany. Martin is just as embarrassed as I am, but I despise him. I shouldn't hate him, but I'm angry in having to be in a baby class with him when I can speak better English than he does. I'm smarter than he is, too, although I'm unable to get all my smarts out on paper yet. The Public School Society is arguing all the time about teaching Protestant ways to Catholic children and all I want to do is to learn.

I have a difficult time understanding what we're praying when we're forced to kneel and pray in the mornings at school. I don't mind being late for school and missing this ritual! I don't want to be with the Protestants if I can help it, not after the cruelty they inflicted on us in Ireland. I thought it would be different in this country, but it doesn't seem to be much different when it comes to being despised by Protestants, whether they're American or British. We're hated here for being Irish and Catholic, just like we were in Ireland.

New York City schools are crowded with immigrants who don't know enough English to understand their lessons. The teachers said that until we learn strong skills in English, we are required to sit in the baby classes. It's very difficult because we are adjusting to a new country that has strange ways and a lot of hate. I can speak English better than most immigrants, except the one or two from England. We always spoke Irish in our home in Ireland, but we had to learn English in the national schools and we spoke it in the marketplace. I think of Ireland with sadness as I sit uncomfortably at my desk. My heart aches when I think of our small cottage home. I'm confused about being in America, but there are times I've felt exciting possibilities exploding in my mind. There are no big open fields to run through to pick wildflowers and berries, and we don't sit around the hearth with our neighbors and tell stories. On the other hand, I've been inside a bakery and have seen coins flying around the streets. Sean is my best friend and there is something magical every time I step foot on the streets to sell papers to people from all over the world.

"Time to sing, boys and girls! Time to sing, 'My Country, 'Tis of Thee!'" our teacher, Mrs. Drake, instructs, taking a pitch pipe out of her desk to play the opening notes.

We scramble out of our desks, boys going to one side of the room and girls to the other side. I struggle to remember the words and I'm perplexed because the music to this song is the same as the music to the British national anthem. The difference is that the lyrics aren't, "God save our gracious Queen, Long live our noble Queen." When we sing, "land where my fathers died, land of the pilgrims' pride," I nearly choke. This isn't the land where my fathers died, and who are the pilgrims? I wonder. And then I think that life is so rough in America, maybe my father will die here.

We must sing about America now, immigrant and native alike, but it is the native's song, not my own. Singing this song reminds me of when we had to recite a poem in school in Ireland about being proud little English children. We were dominated by the English although we were Irish, but we had to pretend to be happy English children. Mam and Da resented our attending the national school in Ireland and when they had extra money, they paid the traveling Irish schoolmaster to come and teach us at home. And here I am now singing about being an American, but I don't know if I really am an American or if I want to be an American. Mam and Da know about this song, for I've been trying to memorize it at home. They don't protest me singing this song about America being my country because it was America that let the Irish in when the Famine and the English pushed us out.

I sing loudly the verse, "Let music swell the breeze, and ring from all the trees sweet freedom's song: let mortal tongues awake, let all that breathe partake; let rocks their silence break, the sound prolong."

This verse has nothing to do with being an American, Irish, or German child and it makes me tingle all over when I sing it. I can picture all of us from every part of the world singing so beautifully that the trees, rocks, and wind sing with us. Maybe someday I will become a happy American child, I think, but then I remember the agents in the quarantine station when I first arrived. My eyeballs were rolled around in my head, my hair was pulled and tugged, and the stern faces of the agents inspected every inch of my body. My thoughts fly around my head as I try to sing, but soon the song is over and I hurry to tuck myself back into the seat at my small desk.

"Nora McCabe, please stand before the class and recite a piece from memory," our teacher commands.

I've forgotten that Mrs. Drake asked me to prepare a recitation! I've only been thinking of selling newspapers, but if I don't show her I can speak English well, I'll never get out of this baby class.

I must remember, I tell myself. I will remember, I think, as my cheeks warm with excitement and fear. Words come to me that have been hidden in my heart since I was a wee child and I decide to use them. It won't matter that I don't have something new memorized. I stand up awkwardly and slowly walk to the front of the class. I'm sure that the class will laugh at me for my dress and speech. My face must be as red as a strawberry when I begin to speak,

> Ireland is Ireland through joy and through tears,
> Hope never dies through the long weary years.
> Each age has seen countless brave hearts pass
> away,
> But their spirit still lives on in the men of today.
> (Old song, author unknown)

I almost say that their spirit still lives on in the women of today, too, but I stick to the words of the poet. Some of the dirty faces of the children sitting at their desks break into warm smiles when I finish. I'm especially proud in front of the "Snitcher," a boy who is also a newsie and lives with Sean in his lodging house. He is called the "Snitcher" for telling lies about others that land them in jail. He told Sean that he wants to learn to read so he can sell more papers. He is going to be a newspaperman himself and do the writing instead of the selling. He's as mean a lad as he is ambitious.

"Go to your Irishmen's sidewalk," the Snitcher yells across the room. "No Irish need to read if they stay there." I know that "Irishmen's sidewalk" is a slur of hatred against us, and it means that we should stay on the sidewalk that is in front of our tenements and not walk anywhere else.

Mrs. Drake takes out a long snapping ruler from her desk drawer and it whistles in the air before it comes down upon the Snitcher's bulky hand. The Snitcher is known and feared on the streets of Five Points and he is not one to be reckoned with, but not here in our school room with Mrs. Drake in charge. He pulls back his hand because of the sting from the ruler, but it is clear that his pride stings more. His face reddens with anger and he gets up from his desk, purposely knocking it over before running out the door.

I stand embarrassed in front of the class trying to smooth out the wrinkles in my dress. I had been proud to recite my poem in English and now I'm wondering if everyone feels like the Snitcher. I hate this American school! Tears come to my eyes as I remember the schoolmaster in Ireland when he visited our village and homes a few times a year. We cheerfully clustered around him, eager to learn. The schoolmaster taught in the Irish language and I never felt shame for being Irish. Only once do I remember feeling shame because my Da had to pay a famous schoolmaster and poet with a small coat and a candle instead of money.

Da lectured me after I complained. "They speak English in Dublin and along the east coast in Ireland, but we'll be speaking just a few English words, and these will be out of necessity only. It will be the Irish language that you'll be speaking in my house. Never forget that your great-grandparents were forbidden to read and write. And when they sought the learning, they met out of doors in a sodden house scooped out of the sides of the earth like moles, like animals, to receive the seeds of knowledge. Everything Irish was forbidden by our British masters. But your grandparents learned the call of a bird from a far-off lake as well as their ancient tongue. You will be doing the same in my house!"

And I remember Mam protesting. "They need to go to the national school, Eoin. It doesn't cost us so much as the traveling schoolmaster and they will have more opportunity."

Da protested louder. "The British have come and tried to teach us their ways. They have scorned us!"

Mam wouldn't give up. "My family in Dublin, Eoin, spoke English, and they were as Irish as you are!"

I remember Mam running out the door in tears after she said this to Da. She could speak English well and Da spoke good English, too, but he insisted that we only speak Irish in our home.

Mrs. Drake brought my mind back to the present. "Nora McCabe, you've recited well. You may sit down, child."

"Mrs. Drake," I say, my hands shaking while I try to keep them still, "why do the people of this country hate the people from mine?"

I look out at the students and notice that they are as poor as I am. They sit wiping their noses with the backs of their hands, some of their heads are bowed in tiredness on their desks, and others have been alerted to the entertainment of my plight. I drop my head onto my chest and I'm glad Da isn't here to see me. How disappointed he would be to see me hang my head.

Mrs. Drake comes to me and puts her arm around my shoulders and leads me back to my seat. "No, Nora, only some people hate the Irish, but they also dislike anyone who is different from them. If they looked inside themselves, perhaps they would see they do not like themselves either."

I can't concentrate on my studies for the rest of the day because I'm worn out from selling papers and from the scuffle with a dog and gang of boys. I keep daydreaming about my school days in Ireland. They had been full of the smells of heather and the poetry that sang its way into our childish hearts and minds. Maybe in Ireland all we'd ever become would be farmers with no big ambition like the Snitcher's. Yet we'd still recite the poetry of our childhood from the schoolmaster and make music and dance around the hearth.

"I had no stockings or shoes for my feet most of the time in Ireland," I think sadly, "but wasn't I merrier in my heart!"

Chapter Five

NORA LISTENS TO LANGUAGES OF THE WORLD

"What, you are stepping westward?" "Yea."
—Twould be a wildish destiny,
If we, who thus together roam
In a strange Land, and far from home,
Were in this place the guests of Chance.
—William Wordsworth, "Stepping Westward"

I can't keep myself from running as we leave school. Children around me shout to one another in their native tongues. We have the same desire to be freed from our small desks to run and play in the streets, although we walk in different directions to go home. It is both confusing and thrilling to hear different languages jumbled together, and if I listen closely to this mishmash of tongues, a picture of sound forms in my mind. It is a sound shaped and patterned by the trills, clicks, and rolls of the various languages spoken. I imagine this sound as a field of wildflowers touched by a gentle, yet strong, wind that bends each flower into one colorful dance. When we are in school, our distinct voices are hushed and surrendered to American ways when they are placed over our minds. What would the song, "My Country, 'Tis of Thee" sound like if it were recited in each of our own languages? Which language would finish first? I wonder.

"We've escaped, thanks be to God!" utters a voice next to me. I turn to see a tall skinny girl dressed in a ragged, but colorful, dress. She has large blue eyes and a mouth like a smooth pink pebble, and her head is surrounded by a mop of tangled red hair.

"I'm Mary," the waif says.

"I'm Nora. Do you not like school, Mary?" I ask.

"Yes and no would be my answer. We've escaped for a few hours, anyway," Mary sighs, "no more feeling like a piece of cork stuck in a bottle!"

I smile at her wit.

"And ye must be from Ireland, too," I remark, "and speak in our own language."

She shakes her head, "I only know the greetings and the counting in Irish. I was born speaking English." I laugh because I know that no one is born speaking any language.

"And what county might you be from, Mary?"

"I've come from Dublin nearly two years ago and now it's this country I'm glad for, not Ireland. I sing praise to America!" she proclaims and then laughs. I envy her wholehearted confidence in this country because I am only halfhearted in my feelings.

We walk together along the noisy streets engrossed in our new friendship. Mary is secretive about her life in Dublin, but I don't mind. Everyone wants new beginnings and I like Mary's humor and spunk. It reminds me a bit of my own.

"Your reading today was lovely, Nora," she says.

"Thank you, but I . . ."

"Shhh," Mary interrupts, "don't give a compliment away to a dark room of your mind. You're a smart girl, 'tis clearly to be seen!"

"How old are you?" I ask.

"I'm not nearly the age of a lady and I'm not as young as a colt," she says with a glimmer in her beautiful blue eyes that reflect possibility.

"You won't tell me your age, then? I'll tell you my own, anyways. I'm fourteen and should be fairly grown up, but at least I don't cry as much as I used to. My tears dried up in the salty air on my way to America!" I don't tell her about the tears that sprung from my eyes all morning long.

"I suppose I'm old enough to marry," Mary says, sighing again. "I'll be sixteen soon."

"And why would ye be wanting to marry?" I ask, dumbfounded. "There's nothing but hardship and drudgery. I only wish to take care of myself and, of course, my Mam and Da. I never want to be married!"

Mary's cheerful face suddenly tumbles into sadness. "If I marry, I can leave the orphanage."

"Oh," is all I can say, surprised and sad. Mary must live in one of the institutions for orphaned children, and I've heard it's worse than living in a tenement building crawling with people and rats. At least I have my mother's care covering my fears at night and my Da's pride in me. I suddenly feel affectionate towards Mary and want to share with her the plan I came up with when I was daydreaming in school today. Working as a newsie has become a dangerous profession, and after today's scuffle with the dog and boys, I need to find a new job. Sean will be disappointed because he says that once you're a newsie you'll always be a newsie. I will always be a newsie in my heart, but it's time to move on to bigger and better things.

"I'm going to give up being a newsie, Mary," I blurt out. As soon as I say this, I feel terribly disappointed in myself. How can I give it up?

"Are you interested in finding work with me? We can work every afternoon after school and we'll make bundles of money together!" I ask hurriedly so as to bolster my decision.

Mary stops walking and grasps my hands. "You're a newsie? So am I!"

I'm astonished that Mary also dresses up as a boy to sell newspapers. She might have been one of the boys fighting in front of the *Sun*.

"Were you at Printing House Square this morning?" I ask.

"I was sleeping like a baby in the back of the building and missed the papers when they were set out."

"You and I were rivals in the newspaper business just this morning, but here we are now becoming good friends!" I pull my hands away from Mary and clap them in delight. I'm grand now to be having another Irish friend to confide in. Maybe we'll be finding work together on the streets, too. I miss Maggie, my dear friend I traveled with on the *Star*. My foolish and beautiful Maggie fell into romance on our journey and then married after arriving in New York. The last I heard from her she was moving with her husband, Robert, to England. Of all places! But no matter, here is Mary now, and I'm sure we'll become the best of friends!

"Thanks be to God for your friendship, Nora!" Mary exclaims, reaching to clasp my hand again as we walk down the street.

Chapter Six

A Surprise for Da

The promised land flies before
us like the mirage . . .
—Henry George

I say goodbye to Mary and try to avoid being trampled as I make my way home. I am pushed into the street a few times and nearly get struck down by fancy carriages carrying important people. Once I saw a carriage plow into a group of children crossing the street. A boy's leg got caught in the spoke of the wheel and the driver shouted out curses at him instead of helping him. Later, I heard that it was the boy's uncle driving that carriage and he didn't have an ounce of care for his own.

There are thick layers of soot caked on my face. It happens all the time even if I begin the day with a thorough scrub. The dirt is darker here in America than in Ireland and it covers my pale skin and freckles after being out on the streets all day. My Da says I'm beginning to look like one of the colored people living near us. I had never seen a human being with such dark skin before coming to America, not even in Cork City. When I first laid eyes on a colored woman here in Five Points, I wondered what had caused her skin to be as black as molasses. Now I know that it was God Himself

41

who caused it and I'm used to their black velvety skin now. I love to look at the children with their hair as black as coal, wiry, and shiny with colorful ribbons in them. I don't know where they get their coins to buy ribbons, for they are as poor as we are. They don't like us Irish and we don't tolerate them too well, either. Mam said she met a woman from Sligo, her skin white as cream, who married a colored man with skin as dark as night.

I climb the steps of our tenement building and walk right into our apartment because no one remembered to lock the door. It's a good thing because I've forgotten my key, but I'm wary someone may have come to steal my dresser! I leap through the room to touch it and place the newspaper inside that I've saved for Da. I look around the room to make sure nothing else has been tampered with. Then I rinse my face with the dirty water still sitting in the kitchen and lie down next to the dresser. I can hear a gang of boys playing stickball and hitting one another with the broom handle on the street outside our building.

I miss Ireland something fierce when I lie next to the dresser and listen to the sounds of the city. I long to hear the wind's whispering songs and the cry of the curlew in the night. I'd no longer complain of the dampness if I were home again! Our clothing in Ireland was scrubbed white, but here our clothes lines are full of grey linens hanging overhead in the alley between tenements. We may scrub them white, but they turn grey on the lines. And how it smells in this new country! The children smell worse than the pigs that roam the streets. Never would we be allowed to ramble in Ireland like we do here in New York. The adults have their serious businesses and work to go to, but the streets are run by the children. Since I first set foot on the shores of America, I have learned that these streets are the real schoolhouses for young foreigners. We are also called cruel names by some people who have lived here a long time and belong to a group called the Nativist Party. They think they're the fortunate ones because they were born here. They haven't come from Ireland, Germany, or any other far off country, although their parents came before them. They are uppity and self-important, and consider themselves better than the people who have just climbed off the boat half starved or hungering for freedom. Da says most of them are as Irish as we are and they shouldn't be thinking this city is more theirs than ours. We've all been looking for a better life here in America.

I never knew I would miss the color green. Sure, it's to be found here, a lesser green, I'd say, but there's not much in Five Points. There's a patch here and there as I walk the streets, and I nearly go into a trance as I stop to stare at it. I have to get a hold of myself or someday I'll be carted off to the lunatic asylum. The asylum is for the poor souls who go stark raving mad living in Five Points. The green patches make me think of the *sidhe*, an Irish word for fairies. I asked Mam if they lived here in America, but she said that carrying on too much about fairies is *pishoguery*, which means superstition. She said that I'd better be getting myself some holy water to ward off the *Amadawn*, the fool of the fairies who can drive a person to madness. I'm confused by my Mam sometimes! How can she believe in the Amadawn and not the fairy mounds?

I want to meet new friends, but Mam won't allow me on the streets to play games with the other children. She said that it wouldn't be right having our different tongues getting all twisted together. She insists that there would always be a fight because it is like mixing oil with water trying to play games with people who speak different languages. Da doesn't mind me playing on the streets, and when Mam isn't home, I've been learning how to play stickball. A few days ago, I was told that it was a boys' game and girls couldn't play. I was getting ready to hit a ball with the broomstick when my hair fell out of my cap. If my hair had stayed up in my cap, I'd be out there now playing with them! It isn't fair, dang it all! Girls play beanbag toss with little bags filled with cherry pits that their mothers sew, but I'd rather be playing stickball with the boys. Sometimes I watch children playing from the window and wish Mam wasn't so strict about me mingling with people different from us.

There are strange musical sounds in the background of the cries of the boys playing stickball. It must be floating in from the fairy world. The fairies do live here in America! I sit up to listen more intently. The *seanachies*, the storytellers in Ireland, told us that the fairies make a special kind of music called *planxty*. Da says it's possible the fairies are here, too, but Mam says we need the Holy Spirit. I think having as many good spirits as possible, all coming from God, of course, is the best way. And don't I know that the fairies come from God! As soon as I sit up, the sounds vanish! I lie down again and try to sleep, but all I can think of is Ireland. This thinking makes my heart heavy, as if I might not be able to get up, walk, or move my body because my heart weighs me down. How strange that the memory of hunger pains makes me homesick, too, because I lived through them with my family and neighbors. And now many of these people are gone forever. Oh, my Kate! I begin crying from deep within the well of my heart. It must be that the tears have dwelled there and made my heart heavy. I cry so hard that I think I won't be able to stop as I continue thinking about Ireland and Kate.

I also miss the melody of the red-winged blackbird because it has been replaced by the shrill crowlike voices of the street gang boys, the whistle of a cop, or an organ grinder cranking on his hurdy-gurdy.

As I ponder these things and empty my heart of its tears, I fall asleep and dream of playing with my new friend, Mary. In my dream, we're back in Ireland wearing crowns of braids filled with flowers and walking together to a Cake party at the O'Connells'.

"Nora?" Da wakes me from my happy dream.

I open my eyes when I hear his familiar voice. I sense playfulness in him and jump up quickly from the floor. I want to recapture this part of him I haven't seen since we left Ireland. I look into his dark circled eyes, but they appear to have lost their keen greeting to life.

"I've been napping and dreaming," I tell him, reaching inside the cupboard of the dresser to pull out the newspaper, placing it in his hands.

Da unfolds it very carefully. His lips curl up into a smile.

"Bless you, Nora, thanks be to God for your tender heart!" he says. "Your Mam will read it, too, and maybe there'll be news about Ireland! When the Famine finishes killing the Irish in answer to British prayers, we'll escape this city! And then, by the vengeance of God Almighty, we'll return and send the likes of them jumping off the Cliffs of Moher." He stops talking and looks somberly into my face.

"Where did you get this paper? I hope you've not spent the bit of money you made helping your Mam."

"I still have some left," I answer. "What time is Meg and Mam coming home?" I quickly change the subject, "I have something for all of us!"

Da sits down at the table in the kitchen and motions for me to come and sit on his lap. My body is small and slender, although I'm nearly fourteen and too old to sit on a father's lap. I can't tell Da this and hurt his feelings because he wants to protect me. He is also missing Kate. I see it in his eyes when he looks far off. He saw her die and then buried her in the world of the sea and he'll never be the same because of it.

None of us will ever be the same since the Great Hunger. Da has been saying to Mam, Meg, and me that he wants to give us all better food and clean air to breathe than what we inhale in this city. He knows I'm running through the streets of New York and it must worry him. I reach up and touch his face for a moment and then fold my hands in my lap and rest on his chest. In Ireland, Da was just a poor farmer, but he was also a poet and fiddler. Here he is only a sweeper. A sweeper of the bank, a sweeper of the streets, and maybe he is sweeping all his painful memories of Ireland away as he works. A few times after I sold all my newspapers, I didn't go to school. Instead, I went to the bank where he works and hid behind a building to watch him. What a hard job to clean up the dung and garbage in the streets, but as I watched him, I noticed him smiling to himself. I think he was happy to be doing something that mattered. In Ireland, he was half starved and the British had him building useless roads. Here he is ridding the city of refuse and dreaming about the future, and I'm certain he's writing his poetry in his mind. I pray for him to be doing so. I want to tell him he isn't just a sweeper, but that he's my special Da, our Da, and the husband of Marion, his Irish queen. He told me that when he sweeps the floors of the bank and cleans the streets in front of the bank, he listens to so many foreign words that he feels the Irish tongue is leaving his head. I told him his tongue would always be Irish no matter how many languages he listened to every day.

I want to pull out the old playfulness in my weary Da, but don't know what to do. I climb off his lap to get the bread from Helga's bakery out of the dresser. I have hidden it to surprise my family this evening when we'd all be together again, but now I hand it to Da. He needs something to rid him of his gloom and I can't wait for Mam and Meg to come home. He takes it from me and smiles as he touches the strange looking shape and feels the texture of the bread. When Da receives his pay at the end of a week, he always brings it home to Mam. He never stops at any of the vendors, shops, or pubs along the streets. Even the grocer has a swill to sell his brew to his paying male customers, but Da hasn't touched a drop since coming here. Although he isn't the same, I've seen glimmers of the old Da hopping in and out of him recently. He said he doesn't want to speak to anyone if he doesn't have to, only to the few Irishmen who haven't soiled themselves with rage and drink. I think he's afraid of giving himself away as a fool, "an Irish fool," he'd say, in the eyes of the Nativists. The Irish people are thought of as ignorant and dirty, and Da has a lot of pride. He doesn't say any of this to me, but I've figured it out with the old soul I've grown since leaving Ireland. Mam is different altogether and able to go to the market and speak to anyone she pleases. She doesn't seem to mind the taunts and is always able to hold her head up high as she does her shopping.

"My, Nora, this bread isn't like our Irish bread," Da says, squeezing it in his hands.

"The crust is hard on the outside but the bread soft as feathers on the inside," I say, "but why is it so yellow?"

"They put lots of eggs in it," he explains. "They have the money for the eggs and charge us three times what it costs them to buy the eggs and make the bread."

Da lays the bread down and begins to sing:

I would climb the high hills of the land,
I would swim to the depths of the sea,
For one touch of her lily-white hand,
Ach ar Eirinn ni neosainn ce h-i,
("Ireland over all")

When Meg and Mam arrive home exhausted, we go for clean water and make a meal to eat with the delicious bread I have brought home from the bakery. No one asks me where I got the special bread because they're all too tired and weary. My family doesn't really want to know the frightening details of my street wanderings. They must understand that the ordeal on the coffin ship has prepared me for the streets of New York, although Mam still forbids me to mingle with other children and Da daily warns me of the dangers on the streets. Da and Mam once clung to Kate and begged her to live and then watched her die. Now they are letting go of me and watching me live.

Chapter Seven

A MOUSE, LAUGHTER, AND DA'S NEWS

For who else would dig, and delve, and drudge,
and do domestic work, and make canals and
roads, and execute great lines of Internal
Improvement! Irishmen both, and sorely
puzzled too, to find out what they seek.
—Charles Dickens, *American Notes*

"I'm worried about Da," I whisper to Mam so Da won't hear me. "He sits at the kitchen table after coming home from work and stares." She ignores me and continues to work on her sewing.

Summer is nearly over and I'm not looking forward to school starting again. It seems like yesterday when Mary and I made plans to sell goods on the street together. My family and I are still living in two cramped rooms, but we recently asked the landlord if we could move to an apartment with three rooms. Mam wanted to take in boarders so we could have some extra money. The landlord was furious and gave us a mighty lecture.

"What have you to complain about? I have families of eight who rent out two rooms! Your kind is making money that is due me because you take in renters and then crowd yourselves in filth that costs me in the end because I have to run the vermin out of the building."

I know all about the vermin—mice bold enough to come out during our evening meal or when we're sleeping. One of the girls that Meg works with told her a horrid story about a rat that ate a baby's big toe in the middle of the night when everyone was sleeping. When Meg came home and told us this story, I couldn't sleep, but Mam says we're too clean for the rats to be bothering with us when there's plenty of filth elsewhere in Five Points. The landlord has threatened to increase our monthly rent from $8.00 to $12.00 and evict us if we take in a boarder. The girl who told Meg about the rat story wanted to come and board with us, but Mam said we can't take the chance of the landlord finding out and evicting us. Besides, the girl is Italian and Mam said she doesn't want her strange ways in our home. The landlord says we're the lucky ones and I suppose we are. He's keeping an eye on us now, fearing we'll bring someone in to help pay the rent. In May of next year, people all over the city will move to new and better apartments. They do this every year and Mam said we'll move into a three-room apartment, but by then I hope the Famine will be over in Ireland and we'll be returning home.

I nudge Mam with my elbow and nod in Da's direction as he sits at the table looking at absolutely nothing. I want her to see the sadness in him that I can see, but Mam, although weary herself, will never admit to either one of them being sad.

"On my oath, Nora, your Da needs rest," she whispers.

I'm sitting next to the dresser and she is sitting on one of the kitchen chairs that she pulled over near me.

"His body is resting and his mind is thinking about tomorrow's doings," Mam says.

I know I should say no more, but we've been through too much to have him end up staring at nothing every evening.

"But he hardly talks at all! Not about going back to Ireland or moving somewhere else like he used to talk about when we first moved here. He doesn't sing and he doesn't play his fiddle. He doesn't care if we move anywhere. He doesn't care about us anymore! You were the one who asked the landlord if we could move to a bigger place. Da knows we'll never be leaving this bloody city!" I whisper angrily, leaning back against the dresser knowing that I have stepped over the line.

Mam sighs and puts away her stitching as the dark of night wipes away her light to see by. I'd never be allowed to speak disrespectfully to my parents when we lived in Ireland. I wait for a scolding from her, but then Meg walks through the door from her day at the factory. Poor Meg looks exhausted and her body is still thin from our hungry days in Ireland. Her dress, a checkered green and black, is more black than green, having not received the washings it should have since our aunt made it for her when we first moved here. We have to do our wash on a weekend and dry the clothes on the roof of this rickety old building. People living in the back of the building hang their clothes on the pulley lines, but we have to stand guard all day to wait for our clothes to dry on the roof so no one steals them. Meg's face is brooding and drawn and I wonder about the big notions she always had about herself. I watch as her lips manage to curve a smile for Mam. She looks a moment at Da, but then turns back to Mam, ignoring me altogether.

"'Tis an early night for me, Mam, for I've lost the job. I walked right out! I couldn't tolerate the advances of the manager who thought me to be an easy one." Meg collapses onto an old blanket lying on the floor next to Mam's chair. Mam doesn't act surprised or say a word about this news from Meg. It seems nothing surprises her anymore. I can see that she is mulling over my tart remarks and Meg's plight that will now cause us to have less money and less food. She glances at Da and I think she must know that I am right about him. He has lost his spark for life and is staring straight ahead as if Meg never came through the door and told us her bad news.

No one makes tea or prepares for the evening meal. I hear Da's breathing now and then as he taps the table with his fingers. He continues to stare as Mam puts away her sewing. And then both Meg and Mam sit and stare! Their faces are growing dim and dark as the night creeps into our apartment and into our hearts. We only have one candle that we are not supposed to use too often because candles cost a pretty penny. The landlord said we shouldn't use them at all because the building could go up in flames because it's made of dry timber, but it's all we have to see by at night. We must make this one last, especially now that Meg is out of work, but I don't care. I have to light the candle and shoo away some of the darkness that is swallowing up my family. I rouse myself up from the floor in the dark to see if I can find the matches I picked up from the street yesterday. When I find them, I light the candle and everyone turns to look at the light. Their faces are aglow with the softness of hope, but they say nothing. I'm sure the candle will help them think of better tomorrows, but just then a mouse scampers across the floor right by Mam and Meg. No one moves or cares! At least it isn't a rat, I think, and wonder if Paws is climbing up and down the stairs in the building looking for mice when they're right inside our apartment. Where is that cat when I need him! I chase the mouse into a corner and then grab it by the tail and swing it in the air.

"Dinner anyone?" I ask, and my family begins to laugh. The room fills with lightness that pulls the shade over the gloom in the room. The light of the candle has done its work. I twirl in a circle with the poor mouse before I throw it out the open window into the street where a gang of boys are clamoring for importance below. I look outside in the darkening twilight to see where the mouse has landed and pray it won't get hurt. The poor thing has fallen onto a wide-brimmed felt hat of one of the boys. The other boys begin pointing and laughing at him. The mouse, though dazed, jumps from the boy's hat and scampers into an alley where probably Paws or some other cat will chase it. Da, Mam, and Meg have gotten up to look out the window, too, and we're all laughing. Maybe we shouldn't be laughing too hard because there might be families around here desperate enough to eat a mouse or two. Maybe someday it might be us wanting a mouse for dinner! But no, not tonight. The mouse has fed us with humor and lightness, and for that I'm thankful.

The candle flickers in the drafty apartment and the handbills that are pasted to the wall for insulation are beginning to curl. One is half off the wall and fluttering in the breeze from the open window. I shut the window and stick the page back onto the wall.

"True Democrats Meet Here," it says. I don't know whether we are Democrats or not, or what the word actually means. What I know is that the nights are growing colder and we need to decide what to do before winter comes again and the snow becomes our blanket in this room where there is not enough coal to heat it with. As the laughter over the mouse disappears and the candle fights the windy dark night, Da suddenly speaks to us with resolution. "I'll be going out West to make us some real money. I've heard there's an Irish gang led by a lad named Macky mining some gold in California."

I'm familiar with this tone of voice in Da and I know to take it seriously. It was this very tone he used in Ireland when he announced that we'd be sailing for America.

Later, after everyone is sleeping, I lie awake next to the dresser and make my own firm decision. I will not stay here in this city without my Da. He promised that he would take me home to Ireland, but now he'll be going further away from Ireland, across this wild country, alone without any of us with him! I will go home to Ireland myself. I will go and make a way for all of us to someday live there together again. I don't sleep the entire night as I think about my family and what I must do.

Our Meg is young and smart, and although she is tired and worn out, she'll find work again here in Five Points. She'll endure the flirtations, crude remarks, and more resignations, to be sure. She is as beautiful as a soft velvety red rose, but she is also as hard as nails.

We received a letter from our cousin in Ireland who said that he's able to feed his family with the money we've been sending to him. I can go and stay with him until I get settled in our home again. My cousin has no idea that we sometimes have to go without proper food here to send him this money. It will be best for me to go back to Ireland and make sure we can survive as a family there. Isn't it up to all of us to survive and leave word for the next generation that it can be done—that life can go on breathing, eating, and loving no matter how much suffering there is?

Maybe Da is right about my old soul. I must have grown ten feet in my soul, although Mam is quick to tell me that I still possess the foolishness of dreams that young people have. She said we carry these dreams into troubles if our parents aren't there to pack them away until we are mature enough for them. I told her that these foolish dreams are what is needed for us to find hope to carry into our tomorrows.

"You're full of *brilla-bralla*, Nora," Mam told me that day. Then I made the big mistake of telling her it would be wise for her to say I was full of nonsense and not *brilla-bralla* as no one in America would even know what she meant.

"I'm talking to me own child, not everyone in America. If I was talking to them, I wouldn't use the Irish words they wouldn't know. Ye are getting too uppity since we've come to this city." And when she used the word, "ye," I cringed, for I've been trying not to use it so much here in America, but maybe I'd better be keeping my 'ye this and ye that's' if I'll be returning home! The manner of speaking here is flat and dull and I'm afraid that if I stay too long, I'll end up speaking this way, too. I won't because I'll be returning home to Ireland very soon. I finally sleep at 4:00 a.m., the same time I used to be going out the door to sell newspapers with Sean. No more, life is changing rapidly and I have to be catching up with it.

Chapter Eight

Everything Is Changing

All Europe is coming across the ocean—all
that part at least who cannot make a living
at home—and what shall we do with them?
They increase our taxes, eat our bread
and encumber our streets, and not one in
twenty is competent to keep himself.
—Philip Hone

"I've looked for you all summer," Sean says as he approaches me on the street. His clothing looks more tattered and dirty since the last time I saw him.

"You could have made a bunch of money selling newspapers," he says harshly.

The warm giddy look Sean used to wear just for me is now gone. I'm not going to tell him I worked with Mary on the streets all summer instead of working with him. He sidles up to me, and as we walk, the rough texture of his old jacket rubs against my bare arms. It's September and there's a brisk chill to the air and I don't have a coat or jumper to keep me warm.

"You're different," Sean says.

"We're children, I suppose, and still growing, so we're sure to be different all the time," I answer.

"No, it ain't that. You've put on airs."

"You've seen me but five minutes! How can you see that I have airs?"

"It's in the air around you." Sean skips ahead and then turns and stops directly in front of me. We both stand on the side of the street looking at each other. Does he know about my secret?

I haven't told anyone about my plans to go to Ireland. If I talk about it, my old fear will come upon me and I won't be able to go. I'm planning to leave in the spring and this means that I'll have to work hard all winter. I'll have to find work as a domestic servant or with one of the seamstresses I know in Five Points. It will be too cold to be peddling my wares on the streets in the winter. Lately, Mary and I have been selling hot steaming corn on the streets. We tried selling apples and the flat gingerbread cakes called bolivars, but we didn't make any money. We worked for an old Irishwoman who smoked a pipe and took all the money at the end of the day. She would give us the bolivars and apples to take home, but no money! Now we're "corn girls," and we've been making a lot of money. I'm right proud of myself when I shout out, "Hot corn, hot corn, here's your lily-white hot corn/Hot corn, all hot, just came out of the boiling pot!"

Mary is especially good at selling corn because she knows how to turn a boy's head to look at her sparkling blue eyes and shining red hair. She has a different cry than I have, "Here's your nice hot corn, smoking hot, smoking hot, just from the pot!" She wears a dress that shows off her large bosom that has suddenly popped out of her chest. If Mam knew I was selling corn on the streets with the likes of flirtatious Mary, I might be sent back to Ireland anyway. There's talk that some of the "corn girls" are selling more than corn on the streets of New York. Mam says the girls crying out their wares are really crying out for trouble. She says they end up in houses of prostitution where they die in less than a month from disease or violence. I don't believe it's as bad as Mam makes it out to be. In fact, I've begun to believe my Mam exaggerates and my Da isn't true to his word. Mary says she's met some girls who live in the prostitution houses and they wear fancy red dresses and become very rich. Sometimes I wonder if Mary is tempted when a handsome man offers her his calling card and gives her the going over with his lusty eyes. I wouldn't ever be tempted to make money in a prostitution house, even if it helped me buy my ticket to Ireland. I don't receive the attention Mary gets, anyway, because my bosom is flat and I look like I'm wearing buttons on my chest. My hair isn't the flaming ginger color like Mary's and I've got as many freckles as a spotted hen. Maybe this is God's way of keeping me safe because I've never gotten a calling card from any boy or man.

"I was worried you'd gone back to Ireland, you missing the ole country all the time," Sean says to me, blushing and casting his eyes down. I sure wish he'd get himself some better clothes and try washing the city grime off his face. You'd think that with his family sewing clothes in their home for the factories, they'd make him some new trousers.

"I never said anything about going back to Ireland," I say, worried he knows about my plan.

"No, but you were always complaining about being here and how it's better there, forgetting the starvation and dead bodies. People are always looking somewhere else to make them happy. Nothing better than selling papers in America and finding some happiness with the coins piling up, I'd say."

"A boy has it much easier selling the papers."

"I was with you. I helped you, didn't I? Come back to selling the papers with me, Nora. I'll even make sure you sell more than I do, and I'm practically the king of the newsboys now!" Sean is looking straight into my eyes and it makes me nervous.

"Da's going to California and dig for gold. When he fills his pockets with gold, he'll come back for us and we'll be settling somewhere else other than this city. He used to talk about returning to Ireland, but no more. I'm going to make enough money to go to Ireland myself and I can't make enough money selling the darn papers! Even if you do help me! And I don't need a boy's help. I don't even need Da's help now! I'm going to get back to Ireland on my own. When Da gets rich on the gold in California, he'll bring Mam and Meg to Ireland to be with me."

There, I said it. I let the cat out of the bag to Sean about me going back to Ireland. It actually feels great to have finally shared it with someone. I'm not one to keep my thoughts and feelings all bottled up inside of me. I can't tell Mary because she has a big mouth and will tell everyone she knows. I know Sean will keep my secret. I know it, for he's been a good friend. He's staring into my eyes and I can tell that he's begging me to sell the papers with him again. I won't! I'm free to make my own money without his help or anyone's help! And I won't let on how sad I am over Da planning to leave either, or how terrified I am of returning to Ireland alone on a ship. I begin dancing a little jig, for it feels so good to be free of my secret.

"You're mad, Nora, to be dreaming of Ireland. But if you want to get there, being a newsboy is the best way to make enough money . . ."

"Newsgirl, not newsboy, Sean. And I've got other plans to make money. Besides, I've been making money all summer without selling the papers with you."

Sean looks down at his old boots and then kicks the dirt with his right foot.

"Okay, I'll call you a newsgirl . . . but I think you're still mad not selling the papers with me. What are you selling? Fish? You'll become a smelly fat old monger who screams at passers-by with slimy little ones under yer feet! You'll never get back to Ireland selling the fish on the streets."

"It's none of your business." I start walking and Sean walks alongside of me.

I'm sorry now that I've shared with Sean my plans to go back to Ireland. I think he must be jealous over my adventurous spirit. He talks of big things, like Meg, but he doesn't have the determination to make a change. Selling newspapers! He wants to be a news-boy so much that he'll never become a man! I think he's just upset because he misses me and doesn't know how to express it. I don't like the freckles on him be-cause I have so many on myself, but there's something mighty nice about Sean in spite of all his freckles, and I'm feeling some warmth for him that I've never felt before. If he got himself cleaned up, I think he might even be a handsome lad.

"God with my soul, Nora! After all I've done to help you in the newsboy business. Now it's off to selling fish and marrying a monger . . ."

"You are the mad one, Sean O'Connolly! I've never seen such carrying on in a boy!"

"Do you know any boys? No brothers have ye, only a sister!"

"I have Da and I do believe he counts for a boy!"

"Do as ye please, then!" Sean says, pulling his cap over his eyes and walking ahead of me.

"Wait!" I yell and run to catch up with him. When I do, I pull on his arm and he stops. I can't see his eyes for they are hidden underneath his cap.

"I'm a loyal friend. Ye must believe it. I'm no longer a newsie, but I'll always be around for Sean O'Connolly!" I reach for his hand but he pulls it back, adjusts his cap again, and puts his hands in his pockets.

"There's no 'O' in me name! And I'm not worried about loyalty."

Then he turns and runs away from me. As he jogs down the street, I stand dumbfounded and hurt that he has rejected my friendship. Maybe I've been too harsh with him, but it's too late now, because he has left me standing alone on the street.

After Sean leaves, there's hollowness in my chest that drums sadness into my mind. I fear I'll never see him again and that something terrible will happen to him. I gather my senses together and begin walking down the street in the opposite direction of where Sean ran off to. I don't have time to think about Sean O'Connolly any longer because I have to go to school. I'm afraid it's going to be difficult after his angry departure from me. And I had been eager to go to school today because Mrs. Drake said I'll be going into an older class in a few weeks. She's been reciting some new poetry to us by poets, like Walt Whitman, who live right in New York. I don't understand how a poet could get inspiration from these muddy and filthy streets because the poets in Ireland mine their words from the green and flowering earth. When Mrs. Drake read Mr. Whitman's lines from one of his poems, I wrote it down and tried memorizing it. I was thinking that if he could find glory in this city to write about it in a poem, maybe I could, too. I say aloud Mr. Whitman's words,

> City of the World! (for all races are here),
>   All the lands of the earth make contributions
>   here;)
> Proud and passionate city—mettlesome, mad,
>   extravagant city!
> Spring up, O city—not for peace alone, but be
>   indeed
> Yourself, warlike!
> Fear not—submit to no models but your own O
>   city!

After I had memorized the poem, I recited it to Mary.

"Ye shouldn't be too pleased with this Mr. Whitman. He despises us Irish," she said.

"We're becoming too worried over everyone hating us. Not everyone is a Nativist. I don't think Mr. Whitman is one, do you?" I asked her.

"Read the papers, Nora. He writes ugly words about the Pope sending the Irish to take over America with their religion and pagan ways."

"You don't read the papers, Mary. You're too busy fussing with making yourself beautiful and working all the time."

"My new friend, Mick Murphy, read it in the paper and told me about it. He even pointed Mr. Whitman out to me one day on the street talking to himself." Mary tossed her head back and her red curls bounced haughtily in my face.

That day was the first time I felt anger towards Mary. I wasn't just angry over having my bubble burst concerning Mr. Whitman, but disappointed that she had a new friend who was a boy! But by the time we met up again, I had forgotten about our words over Mr. Whitman, and Mary didn't mention her new friend. As I walk to school, I remember what she said and decide I'm going to ask Mrs. Drake if she can show me the drawing of Mr. Whitman that was in a newspaper she brought into class one day. I won't just memorize his poems, but his face, so that if I happen to see him on the street, I'll ask him about his poetry and his dislike of the Irish.

Later, at school, I find it isn't as difficult to concentrate as I thought it would be because I put Sean O'Connolly right out of my mind. Mrs. Drake is pleased to show me the newspaper with Walt Whitman's picture in it. I study it real hard so I'll be able to recognize him someday on the streets. Mary said he wanders a lot, making up poetry wherever he goes.

After school, I invite Mary to our apartment because I want to convince her that I lived inside my dresser while crossing the Atlantic. I've told her about the fairies who lived there with me, but Mary is too practical and doesn't believe in the old ways and superstitions from Ireland.

"Come along, Mary, the Home won't be missing you. They have too many of the likes of you to keep track of," I joke with her.

Mary laughs and says, "No family to tie me down and isn't it grand that I can run before and after school, all the while the Home thinking I'm in school or working!" Mary tries to be positive about living in an orphanage.

"I'm practically an orphan, too, Mary, with me Da going to meetings all the time about the trip to California, and Mam and Meg working late."

"Ye don't know much about being without a Mam and Da," Mary says, and I feel sorry for saying what I did. I want to hurry to show her our apartment and the dresser. Then I'll make us some tea and we'll pretend we're the grown-ups living there!

"The sun is still glistening on the tall buildings; the birds have all gone to Ireland, but we're here to sing their songs as we walk, Mary!" I try to bring some happiness back into our steps.

We run down the street to where I live, singing and laughing as if our childhood was a normal one. When we reach our building, we can't believe our eyes. Our screams rush out of us like a mighty river because my tenement building has fallen and is leaning onto the next building. The floor we lived on looks as if it has given in to sadness and now sags uncomfortably into the arms of someone stronger. It doesn't look torn up at all, just folded down sideways near the ground while being hugged by a neighbor building. Everyone knows that the construction of these large frame houses is made with cheap, flimsy materials. They were built too fast and on ground that isn't solid. Many of them lean together for support, but it seems our building and the one next to it couldn't find the strength any longer to stand as they did. All I can think of is my dresser being destroyed in the tumble. I look around to see if anyone is coming to the rescue, but the police and firemen haven't arrived yet. There are some people wandering around dazed and drunk, and there are empty bottles of Jim Beam whiskey sitting around the fallen steps. I run towards our tenement building to rescue my dresser.

"Is it safe to go inside?" Mary calls after me.

"I've see them like this all over the city," I answer, "it must be okay. You wait outside while I go in to make sure."

"No, Nora, don't go in, I've a feeling about it. Don't go in!" Mary yells.

I take no mind to Mary's pleading because I have to get to my dresser. Before she can say another word, I climb the narrow and crooked steps to go into the leaning building. When I get inside, I find our apartment and nothing seems different except that the floors are uneven and the dresser has flown to the side of the wall. I yell out the window at Mary, "You can come in, it looks to be safe!"

Mary tries to convince me to come down, but I won't listen.

I open up the cupboard of the dresser and climb halfway in to retrieve my treasures. As I'm gathering my things, I hear an enormous sound of breaking wood and realize the building next to ours can't hold us any longer and it must be crashing to the street. I see lights flash before me as I fall with my dresser, and I wonder if soon I'll be seeing my friend Jack and sister Kate in heaven.

Chapter Nine

WE ARE ALL SEASHELLS

Out of the night that covers me,
Black as the pit from pole to pole,
I thank whatever gods might be
For my unconquerable soul.
—William Ernest Henley, *Invictus*

A horse-drawn steam engine roars onto the street where the tenement building has fallen like a wounded soldier in battle. Wild dogs bark and snap at the curious onlookers who are congregating around the tumbled building.

"Is there anyone inside?" a fireman asks the onlookers. There is concern about a fire starting from stoves that might have been burning in the apartments.

"Everyone's gone to work," someone says.

A small wiry child with black hair corkscrewing around her dirty face is crying and wandering in the crowd of people.

"Is your family in the building?" someone asks her.

The child runs towards a woman walking down the street. The woman lifts her up and asks if her brother is still in their apartment. She puts the child down, grabs her hand, and walks towards a fireman, screaming for him to go in after her son. There are already firemen who have climbed through a window to look for survivors.

At first Mary can't speak for she is in shock. Then she walks over to a fireman, taps him on the back, and points inside the building. "Nora is inside!" she shouts.

The fireman ignores her and walks over to where the other firemen have climbed in. They are going in after the little boy whose mother is standing with her daughter and shouting for help. The side of the building that the McCabes live in has fallen but is not destroyed. Mary makes her way to a window whose side hasn't fallen onto the neighbor building, but is lying on the ground like a gaping mouth looking up at the rest of its parts that have gone somewhere else.

She is trembling and doesn't know whether she should go in to try and save Nora. Maybe she'll find her friend dead! Before she thinks it through, she climbs over the rubble and scrambles inside the window, avoiding the broken glass. She stands up in a still, dark hallway on splintered wood lying around her and looks towards a door where a golden sliver of light is spilling out. Mary clenches her fists tightly by her sides, a habit she has had since moving to New York from Dublin. Her nails cut into her hands and suddenly she feels them being gently pried open and held as she is led towards the door where the light is coming from. She doesn't find it strange that this is happening, but follows the light, opens the door, and inside is a large dresser sitting on its side. Mary's head is filled with thudding beats of dread because she knows this is where Nora is.

The pine dresser has wondrously remained strong and hasn't been destroyed in the fall, although there's a large dent with the blue paint chipped away on one side of it. A sob seizes Mary and she cries out for Nora, but there is no answer. She stands in the quiet apartment and stares at the dresser, unable to move. The dresser is regal in the midst of the shambles, and she understands now why Nora spoke of it so lovingly. Her fear disappears and she rushes to the dresser to move away some debris that is sitting in front of it.

"Nora! Where are you?"

"Here . . . ," Nora answers weakly.

Mary opens the cupboard doors and is astonished to see Nora curled up tightly like a sleeping cat inside. Her knees are up to her chin and her arms are wrapped around them.

"'Tis the fairies that made me small enough to fit inside again, Mary."

"But can you get out now?" Mary asks, kneeling down and reaching for Nora's hand. Nora straightens out her legs first, surprised that they can move, and slowly lets Mary pull her out of the dresser. When she is out, she stands to her feet and clasps Mary to her in a giant hug. She feels soreness on the right side of her body, but other than that, she is excited to be alive and that her dresser is safe. Both she and her dresser are slightly bruised, but both are strong and have endured.

"The fairies led me here, Nora," Mary whispers in Nora's ear.

"And the fairies stuffed me in my dresser to keep me safe, just like when I was crossing the sea. Now you'll believe in the fairies, too, Mary!"

Mary and I walk carefully through the dust and mangle of the building to escape outside. There is noise and confusion everywhere, but I am relieved to be alive. We learn that a little boy was found lying unconscious in his apartment and there is a doctor tending to him. He'll be okay, but in the cellar was an old man who lay sick and dying on the damp floor. Someone said that he died when the floor we lived on fell and crushed him to death. I begin crying and looking for Paws. Mary holds my hand and stays with me while we look for my cat. After a few minutes, a fireman commands us to sit down on the side of the street. We do what he says and Mary tells me Paws will be fine and then hums a melody. Another fireman brings me a cup of water and a blanket for I am shivering. I keep holding Mary's hand and crying for Paws to come home. I'm afraid he was crushed in the hallway! He is always crouching there looking for a mouse to catch because we never have enough scraps to feed him. I am so glad my family wasn't home, but I'm fearful the firemen won't get my dresser out of the building before it catches on fire and goes up in flames!

"Please, God . . . I promise to go to Mass and confess my lying. I promise not to lie to Mam and Da!"

Mary runs off to look for Paws again and then I see my Da running down the street towards me. Oh, how I love Da! I feel immediate safety, but then sadness comes over me when I remember that he is going to California without us.

"Nora! Nora!" Mary is walking towards me with Paws trying to fight his way out of her arms. I try to stand up, but I'm dizzy and sit back down. She places Paws in my arms and he tries to get away because he is frightened by all the noise and commotion. I hold him down on my lap with all my strength while Da comes to me and asks what happened.

"Go get my dresser . . . hurry!" is all I can say to him. "Please, Da!"

Da turns from me to look for help to get the dresser out of the building. He runs to a fireman and points to where our apartment had been. He and the fireman climb through all the broken wood and through a window into our apartment. Minutes later, they come out carrying the dresser, but I notice that the doors of the cupboard aren't on the dresser!

"Da!" I yell, "Ye must get the doors!" I have used the darn "ye" word! I quickly look around to see if anyone noticed, but no one has paid any attention. I don't care. We are all a jumble of tongues right now, not just Irish, and none of us seem to care who is different. We have come across the sea from different lands and have grown sea shells around us to protect the tiny real parts that are left of us. I guess they are the most important parts, and when we suffer together, we're thrown against each other in our different shells. These shells crack, break, and the tiny parts begin to emerge and crawl out tougher than we ever imagined. We are all the same when it comes to suffering and loss, it seems. These thoughts heat up the tears in my head and as I hug Paws to my chest, they fall on his orange head. Then I see Mrs. Filippio come running over with a pot of hot tea and her dirty children carrying tin mugs. It has to be that God lives in the hearts of people from all over the world.

Da goes back inside the building with another fireman and they carry out my cupboard doors, table, chairs, and the rest of our belongings from the apartment. I wonder where we will live now. I sit on the street and am reminded of Ireland when our neighbors' home was torn down by the British because they couldn't pay their rent. Here we are without our home, but at least we weren't forced out by the British. Da stands beside me with his hands in his pockets.

"We might end up at the Home living with you," I say to Mary as she wipes her nose with the back of her hand and sits down beside me.

"We'll be staying with your Aunt Bridget again," Da says. "It might be best while I'm in California."

"There's no room, Da, and you promised not to leave until spring," I answer him.

"There's talk about taking a ship to California now," he says looking away from me as he speaks. He stares into the sky and I wonder if he is wishing he had wings as a bird and could fly away from all of us. We wouldn't be a burden to him then! My real Da, my old Ireland Da, my fiddling Da, seems to have disappeared months ago.

"What about Ireland? The Famine will be over . . . won't it be over by spring?" I ask him.

"We won't be going to Ireland for a long time," he says as his eyes sweep the sky.

Da used to say we'd be returning to Ireland as soon as the Famine was over. He'd be excited about hearing from our cousins living there and hoping things were better. His words have cut me like a knife. I give Paws to Mary to hold and stand up to face him. I pull on his arm to get him to look at me.

"I'm going back to Ireland, with or without you!" I shout in his face. He reaches for me and hugs me to his waist.

"You're a good girl, Nora, a good girl. Everything will be fine, God willing," he says as he clasps me, but I know different. Nothing will be fine until we are together again in Ireland. And when I am there first, he'll have to come. He won't leave me alone in Ireland. I know it right well.

Chapter Ten

A FANCY CARRIAGE

The Crowd, and Buz, and Murmurings
Of this great Hive, the City.
—Abraham Cowley, *The Wish*

Da says that people from County Cork, where we came from, aren't as clannish as people from other counties in Ireland. Cork people are willing to live all over New York wherever they can find affordable housing. There are some who crowd together on one block where Mulberry, Park, Baxter, and Chatham Streets meet. After our building collapsed and was torn down, we moved to this Cork block in the Five Points neighborhood. We stayed with Aunt Bridget again, but she had too many lodgers and it wasn't possible for us to stay permanently with her. After we first moved in, I heard Mam, Da, and Aunt Bridget discussing me and my rebellious ways. They think that if I spent more time associating with people from County Cork, I wouldn't be using the gutter language of the Yanks. Mam told me that Mary was probably a bad influence, being that she came from Dublin. I walked right up to her and stated that she herself came from Dublin and her reasoning didn't make any sense. She scolded me and said I had to lie down by my dresser and stay there or she'd punish me with a switch. I told her there weren't any decent trees in New York to get a switch off of and she screamed at me to be quiet.

After that incident, I sat by my dresser to read after school every day and refused to eat dinner. Aunt Bridget would give me a cup of tea and soda bread after everyone was asleep. Now we've left good hearted Aunt Bridget and settled at the new apartment with one large room and a small room for Mam and Da to sleep in. This apartment is on the fifth floor, the very last floor of the building. The smells of the other floors waft up to either make us hungry or ill, depending on what smell it is that is drifting up. The small room has a low ceiling and can fit two people sitting up or lying down. Mam and Da have to crawl in every night when they go to bed. I still feel most safe when we're all sleeping together in the apartment, but things have changed between Da and me. He hasn't held me on his lap since the time I brought him a newspaper and a sweet from the bakery, nor has he hugged me since our apartment building collapsed. He works all day and goes to his meetings most evenings. Mam and Meg are working at the Stewart Mansion doing domestic work and they said they'd get me a position there, too. I told them outright that I didn't want to work there and have them always keeping an eye on me. Mam said I would be working there now after that remark. I'd rather work with Mary, but she's been rag picking since the weather got cold and we no longer sell corn on the streets.

I've been going to school regularly, too, but Mrs. Drake said that there isn't room for me in the older class until spring and so I'm still stuck in the baby class. I'll be going to school in Ireland in the spring, anyways, but I don't mention this to Mrs. Drake. She is always giving me new poetry to read and trying to encourage me to write my own poetry. I've been coming home after school and sitting next to my dresser to write, but I still get confused and write in both English and Irish. Mrs. Drake said that I must write in English and if I will practice, she will celebrate my poetry by reading it in public at a special school function. I'm not certain if I want the public to hear my poetry. I've grown fond of Mrs. Drake and trust her sincerity, but I'll be ridiculed for my Irish ways when others hear what my heart is beating out on paper. I also miss my friend, Sean, something fierce, because he and I would talk about poetry and everything. I hope he is still saving his money to return to Ireland, too.

It's nearly December now and there are snowflakes as big as my hands falling on New York. I like these flakes, unlike the small ones, because they don't bring the unbearable cold weather. As they gently land on my face, I can feel each part of the flake explode and refresh my skin as I lift my face to the sky. I imagine these diamond sparkles making my freckles disappear and when I catch sight of myself in a shop window, they seem to have faded!

My toes are ice cold as I walk on the windy street to the Stewart Mansion where Mam and Meg are working today. Mam spoke with Mr. Stewart about me coming to work there after school because Meg has met someone who is going to give her a job at a shop. Mam has been doing all the cleaning and laundry with another Irish woman and said she could use my help, but I don't want to wash and press rich people's clothing. I don't care how grand Mr. Stewart is since he came from Ireland and became a success here in America. I don't want to wash anyone's dirty clothing! I have a small sum of money from selling corn, and if it wasn't so bitter cold, I'd still be selling things on the street. There are people selling hats, scarves, and mittens, and I suggested to Mary we should be selling these things, and then we'd be wearing them, too. I have rags tied around my hands to keep them warm and I'm wearing the coat of a dead girl and fear that the same disease that caused her death is inside the lining of this coat and will cause me to die, too. And if it doesn't, I'll be dying from shame. A neighbor brought it over after her daughter had died from a disease called consumption. Mam washed it as best as she could and if I don't wear it, I'll be freezing to death and never make it to Ireland. Last winter, none of us had coats and we nearly froze to death on the streets and even when we were in our apartment. America is much too cold for me. The wind can be strong and mean in Ireland, but it's a familiar kind of cold that I've become friends with, but here in America the cold seems to match the heart of some of the people.

I walk through Paradise Square and stop to gaze at a group of well dressed and high-falutin' people climb out of a fancy looking carriage. The women are wearing boas, the furs around their necks that hang over their velvet capes. They're wearing cabriolet bonnets, the large bonnets with flaring brims. They're dressed like the fancy carriage they have just climbed out of. The men are wearing chesterfields, large overcoats with velvet collars and top hats. A top hat is called a gibus. I'm proud that I, a ragged Irish girl, know all about high fashion in New York even if I can't wear any of it myself. Someday I will, and I'll be bringing fancy clothing from New York and Paris to Ireland. Besides reading poetry after school, I've been studying high fashion as much as possible. On Printing House Square, there's a small grocer who sells *Godey's Lady's Book*. I love to look at this popular women's magazine where all the gorgeous clothes are in color. It has stories in it, too, and I often sneak into the store and read an entire issue in a corner so the proprietor doesn't catch me and shoo me out.

"Look! Isn't he delightful? I knew we'd love coming here today!" screeches one of the rich ladies pointing at a mustached short man wearing so many hats piled on his head that the hats reach up taller than he is. He is shouting out, "Old clo, old clo, any old clo!" He's an old clothes-man wearing layers of used clothing and many hats on his head to sell. He certainly keeps warm on the winter street, but he can only walk at a snail's pace because of how encumbered he is by what he's selling. One of the men in the group walks over to the old clothes-man and pokes his finger into his chest.

"I say, good chap, how much do you get for the fashionable bang-up you're wearing?" He turns to his friends and laughs uproariously.

This meticulously groomed man continues to laugh and push on the old man's chest. The poor man is so loaded down with clothes that he can't keep his balance and tumbles backward and falls. His hats fall off and slide all over the ice on the side of the road. The other people from the fancy buggy are laughing, too, and I have to cover my mouth not to laugh at the poor man who is now struggling to stand up, but is unable to do so because of all the clothes he is wearing. Other people have stopped to stare and laugh, and everyone is having great fun at the expense of the old clothes-man.

"You dandy, you scoundrel . . . ," yells the old clothes-man as he tries to stand. I rush to gather his scattered hats before some children try to get them.

"Here, old man, give me your hand," says another gentleman in the party who is laughing. He helps him up and then I hand the angry old man all of his hats I've picked up. He curses and makes his way down the street away from the crowd who gathered for some lighthearted fun. I shake my tangled mess of curls and wish that I had kept one of the hats I picked up off the street. If I had the money to spare, I'd have bought one of those warm hats. I adore hats for how they look on my head, and how they keep me warm, but I only have a faded and dirty scarf that is now lying on the ground. I let out a deep breath and notice how it floats like smoke in the air. I pick up the scarf and tie it around my head as I stare at the wealthy people who are looking around for some more poor people to laugh at.

These people must be the wealthy ones who come from afar with money in their pockets to visit Five Points and see the sights, as gruesome as they can be. Their gatherings in Five Points are called slumming parties and some of the women come with camphor in their handkerchiefs to put over their noses so they don't have to smell the foul city. Mary said the women are delicate and genteel, but vulgar, to come and stare at poverty. I'm curious and love the fancy clothing, but despise their ways. They remind me of the Protestant landlord families in Ireland.

"Look at the tangle of curls on the little girl's head! And look, John, I've never see so many freckles on one face!" a woman in the party who has taken off her bonnet is saying as she stares at me. I glare at her. Her beautiful black hair is thick and coiled at the nape of her neck with sparkling jeweled combs in it. She begins to laugh and I feel my face redden.

"I'm not little! I am fourteen years old and a young woman," I say as I hide my rag-covered hands behind me.

"And you're a little Irish girl, too," she says, but then adds, "oh excuse me, I meant to say that you're a young Irish woman." The woman walks closer to me and I back away a little.

"The papers say the Irish are demeaning our country, but you couldn't be one of them. You were very kind to help the old man out. Would you like a ride in our carriage? We're headed to the Barnum Museum. Have you heard of it? Can you show us the way?"

The woman is tittering with excitement and the man who had poked at the old man is back inside of the carriage yelling for everyone to hurry up and get in. The man who helped the old man walks over to the woman and smiles at me while he puts his hand on her elbow to lead her back to the carriage. I'm surprised that the lady asked me if I wanted to get inside their carriage. Even the landlords in Ireland had never asked me to come into their carriages or their houses. The scent of roses is on the fancy ladies and is floating over the whole street. People on the street have gone back to what they were doing before the incident with the old clothes-man, but there are a few watching to see if I will get inside the carriage and go with these grand people to the museum.

The man and woman are talking to one another, but I can't hear because there is noise on the street. A peddler yells, "Rags, rags, any old rags" and a chimney sweep cries out, "Sweep o sweep o." I look around in the fading afternoon light at the brightly painted signs on businesses, and their boldness beats on my brain. I smell tobacco smoke, the acrid stench of pig flesh as they crash down the street, and the sweat from the people jostling me as they walk by. But above it all, there is this intoxicating scent of roses coming from the carriage. The man and woman are still standing in front of me and I wonder if I'm dreaming and the fairies have conjured up this loveliness to beckon me to rise above this city and float like the rose perfume above and away.

Chapter Eleven

P. T. Barnum's American Museum

The pave was filled with an eager and laughing
crowd, jostling along and each intent on some
scheme of pleasure for the evening. I felt confused for a long time with the universal whirl.
—Walt Whitman

I feel like Cinderella in her glorious carriage. I am
not dressed for a ball, but I feel halfway to being in the
fairy tale as I ride down the street in style with my new
friends. The sun has just begun to set and it is twilight, the gloaming is what I like to call it, my favorite
time of the day. The horses clip clop rhythmically down
the street as snow falls like flakes of soap to wash
away the city's grime. The salmon-pink sunset casts
its magical hue upon all of us riding in the carriage. I
am feeling a wee bit like a princess until the lady who
invited me into the carriage asks me if I have lice.

"And tell me now, how could there be bugs in this
frozen place? No, I don't have lice," I say to her, my
head held high, my chin up, my back straight, and my
eyes looking straight into hers.

"Well then," she says, smiling at me as she reaches
behind her head and loosens her hair. She hands me
her jeweled comb. "Since you do not have lice, you may
borrow this to wear in your lovely hair."

Before I climbed into the carriage, I had quickly loosened the rags warming my hands, letting them fall to the ground. I have been sitting on my dirty hands next to the man wearing the chesterfield. I pull them out from underneath me and receive the gift from the ungloved silky white hand that is offering me the hair comb. My hands are dirty from the coal I picked up in the morning to burn in our stove and there hadn't been time to wash them properly. I feel ashamed as I reach out and nearly grab the comb from the lady's hand so she won't notice how dirty it is.

"My hair isn't properly brushed . . . ," I say to her. I want to explain, but how? I keep my mouth closed so she won't notice my dirty teeth. I brush them with a wet cloth every morning and evening, but they still look dingy.

"Leave the child be," sighs the man next to me. The other lady grunts and turns to look out at the street.

I fumble as I try to knot my hair at the nape of my neck before adding the comb to it. The jeweled comb falls onto the floor of the carriage. I lean down to retrieve it, but the lady also leans down to pick it up and we bump heads.

"Oh my!" she exclaims. "You have such a hard little head. Here, let me put it in your hair for you," she says as she leans forward and I turn so she can put the comb in my hair. My face reddens with shame to have such delicate and clean hands touching my greasy hair. The man sitting next to me scoots away in his seat and makes a face at the other people in the carriage.

"Now look at you!" she squeals. "With a little tidying up, you'd be the belle of the ball! Would you like to come and live with me? I could give you a job as a domestic in our home . . ."

"Enough!" the man next to me says harshly. "Stop doting on the child. She isn't coming home with us!

Isn't it enough you have brought her into the carriage for a little amusement?"

The lovely woman sits back in the carriage and sighs heavily, her velvety black hair falling to her shoulders in curls. Her eyes are exquisitely blue, like the jewels in her comb. She looks to be older than my Meg, but I can't tell for certain. She folds her arms and smiles at me. I have never in my life felt like I was pretty and here is this beautiful rich lady fussing over me as if I am. The older women in Ireland talk about how to use the flowers from the field to make yourself beautiful, but they don't tell you that you are. To do so would encourage vanity and self love, and this is not pleasing to God.

"I didn't even ask you your name!" she suddenly cries out, clapping her hands together. She acts so silly and light headed in spite of her beauty.

"My name is Nora McCabe."

"And you may call me Lavonia. Have you been to the Barnum Museum, Miss McCabe?"

"I've walked by it plenty of times, Miss Lavonia. I used to sell newspapers on the street and . . ."

"Newspapers? You sold papers like the newsboys?" she asks as she claps her hands again. "How utterly thrilling!"

"It wasn't easy work with the dogs nipping at my heels and some of the toughs trying to steal my money and papers. I had to quit . . ."

"So you must come to work for us then!" she says looking towards the man sitting next to me who is obviously ignoring her.

The carriage comes to a quick halt at the corner of Broadway and Printing House Row. I have never been here past sunset, but it is clear there is no need for the sun to shine anyway. Gas lamps are burning everywhere! I marvel at the intelligence of people who can imitate the brilliance of the sun and cast it onto the dirty streets to make everything glow. I look out the window and even the tattered rags of a group of poor children look clean against the backdrop of P. T. Barnum's American Museum. Da says Barnum's is the greatest tourist attraction in the country. I twist my head around to the bright museum that takes up a whole block. There are giant banners, signs, and huge colorful murals that depict the animals and features within the building. I have never been to the museum because I have not been willing to let go of a dime of my hard earned money to satisfy my curiosity. However, Mary and I went one late afternoon to see hundreds of rainbow colored balloons being released from the top of the museum. P. T. Barnum is a showman and he knows how to give people their money's worth of entertainment. Mary said that she heard there was a diorama of Dublin inside, a real mermaid from Fiji, and many midgets. I've promised myself that before I return to Ireland, I would visit P. T. Barnum's grand museum just once. Now here I am being taken to the museum like Cinderella going to a ball. I hope I won't appear too dirty and ragged amongst the well dressed people inside.

We climb out of the carriage and stand for a moment gawking at the magnificent building. One of the gentlemen is telling the driver of the carriage to take their suitcases to the Astor House Hotel, which is next door to the museum. I have heard about this gorgeous hotel. It's also a block long and has gaslights in every room, as well as indoor bathing facilities on every floor. I can't imagine what it would be like to live in a building such as the Astor House!

"Come dear, we'll take you inside the museum. Mother suggested we go to the Moral Lecture Room to listen to Walt Whitman and some other bores give a talk on whether New York City has become the Gomorrah of the New World."

She takes my hand in her gloved one and the two men and other woman follow behind us. As we enter the building, we are greeted by an overwhelming stench of the hot flesh of animals. Not that the city streets don't have their own terrible odors from the pigs, wild dogs, and horses, but at least there is fresh air coming to give us some relief. Inside the museum, there is no fresh air and there are other animals besides dogs and horses. One of the doormen gives my friend a small bottle of camphor to be used as we tour the premises. Loud band music is playing from the balcony and as I gaze all around me, I feel that I have been taken into another world. New York City is another world from the world of Ireland, and even within New York City there is another world, which I am presently experiencing. Worlds within worlds! How many worlds will I enter in my entire life? Another employee of the museum hands us a flyer that contains a diagram showing where each exhibit and room is. The gentleman, who I assume is Miss Lavonia's beau, opens up the flyer and the rest look over his shoulder. I watch the people streaming through and there is every class and kind filling the building. There are society people, children, black porters, single women, and many tourists speaking in different languages.

"I don't favor listening to Mr. Whitman speak adoringly of the plebeians, nor do I wish to hear him condemning the city for obliterating its past," Lavonia's gentleman says aloud to the others. They all nod and moan in agreement.

"I'd like to hear Mr. Whitman!" I blurt out. They all stare at me for a moment and then Lavonia puts her arm around my shoulders. Her rose perfume mingles with the elephant dung and makes me suddenly feel nauseous and dizzy.

"Wouldn't you like to see the little people? Maybe they're from Ireland. Everyone wants to see Tom Thumb and Lavinia Warren, for they are the tiniest people ever to be married!" Lavonia suggests.

I don't want to offend Lavonia, but it is difficult to hold my tongue. I don't tell her that her name and the midget's name are very similar. I would like to at least take a peek at this Mr. Whitman who writes inspiring words about New York and despises the Irish.

"I've memorized some of Mr. Whitman's poetry and think it might be interesting, but it'll be grand altogether to stay in your company to go anywhere in the museum," I say, but I don't really feel pleased at all. These are wealthy and upper crust society people and I should be grateful to have them befriend me. Shouldn't I? Talk about worlds within worlds. Their world is one I do not know of, but maybe I can enter into it if I play my cards right, as Da would say.

"Go ahead then and recite some of Mr. Whitman's poetry for us, right here and now," Lavonia says, as she leads us over to the side of the room near a wall. People are streaming by and glance over at us as my new friends circle around me with their hands folded in front of them, waiting for me to perform. The two gentlemen look annoyed, as well as the other woman, who is not as pretty as Lavonia, with her light brown, thin hair and curls beginning to straighten and fall out from underneath her bonnet. Her eyes look at me but are somewhere else, nor are they with her friends at this marvelous museum. I don't think I can remember Mr. Whitman's poetry on the spot like this. My hands are sweating and I take off my coat with the velvet collar that is scruffy and gray. I look down at my faded flowered dress with the torn sleeves and feel naked. I look at these people standing elegantly in front of me and realize that when they got dressed this morning, they, too, had to put one arm in one sleeve at a time. They may have been putting on expensive and clean clothing, but they did the same ritual as I did when I put on my old dress. I straighten my back, lift up my head, clasp my hands behind my back, put one foot slightly in front of the other, and think about worlds within worlds.

> The World is too much with us; late and soon,
> Getting and spending, we lay waste our powers:
> Little we see in Nature that is ours;
> We have given our hearts away, a sordid boon!
> This Sea that bares her bosom to the moon,
> The winds that will be howling at all hours
> And are up-gather'd now like sleeping flowers,
> For this, for everything, we are out of tune;
> It moves us not.—Great God! I'd rather be
> A pagan suckled in a creed outworn,
> So might I, standing on this pleasant lea,
> Have glimpses that would make me less forlorn . . .

I stop reciting because I can't remember the rest of the poem and I have memorized only the part I like best. I don't know about Greek gods, and the rest of it I never understood when Mrs. Drake taught us the poem. I smile at my audience and lean down to retrieve my coat, hoping we can now visit this grand museum. There is loud clapping as I stand up and put my coat over my arm. Lavonia and her friends' velvety pads are barely touching one another as they clap, but then I see that all the clapping is coming from people surrounding us who have stopped to listen. My face reddens again and I feel light-headed, but continue to stand erect and still before the crowd circling me. It is possible that I am small enough to scoot between legs to get away! I want to leave Lavonia and her friends and get away from all the people staring at me! As I think of leaving, I realize that I haven't recited Walt Whitman's poem. Mrs. Drake has been teaching us about American poets and she has especially encouraged me to memorize and do recitations. I have been thinking so much about worlds within worlds, the poem by Wordsworth came to me instead of one by Mr. Whitman!

"Oh my, how impressive," Lavonia says, "but it is not Mr. Whitman that you have recited, but Mr. Wordsworth. Not bad for a little Irish girl just off the boat. Don't you think so, everyone?" she asks her party.

A man with a scraggly looking beard and a face with lines that run from his eyes to his mouth as if his tears have coursed their way there so many times they have left marks, approaches our small circle.

"And do you like this new world of freak shows and human wonders, young one?" his booming voice stills the noise in the room. There are titters of laughter and hushed whispers that indicate people recognize this man.

"Well, if it isn't the esteemed Mr. Whitman, the luminary of our fine city!" the gentleman with Lavonia proclaims loudly.

Chapter Twelve

CONVERSATION WITH WALT WHITMAN

> There was a child went forth every day,
> And the first object he look'd upon,
> that object he became,
> And that object became part of him for the
> day or a certain part of the day,
> Or for many years or stretching cycles of years.
> —Walt Whitman

"The world is too much with me, Mr. Whitman. I'm having great difficulty understanding it." He stands before me with light surrounding his head. Does he have an aura or a halo? I stare at him and soon realize that the gaslights in the museum cause his head to appear as if it is glowing. He doesn't say anything for a few minutes and stares at me, too. I'm trembling and fear my knees will buckle.

"But is it here that is too much for you?" he asks as he spreads his arms around the room, as if absorbing all the light of P. T. Barnum's Museum.

"I've not seen much of the museum yet, sir, but just walking in the door has proven to be too much." People standing around us laugh at my remark and then grow silent waiting for Mr. Whitman to speak. I wait for him to address me again and hear a horrible groaning, as if a monster within the bowels of hell is trying to escape. There is more laughter and people point towards the other side of the room where the sound is coming from. Elephants stand listening to Mr. Whitman, too.

"You must see the elephants first then. They, like you, are feeling out of their element," Mr. Whitman says.

"I am not out of my element. I'm only trying to understand my element."

"But do you see yourself as an integral part of this city?"

"What does integral mean? Does it mean important? If it does, I'm here and I must be an important part of this city just because I am here. I don't understand what you mean by these questions. My teacher, Mrs. Drake, encourages us to ask questions and maybe I should be the one asking you about this city."

Laughter mingles with the moans of the elephants and I'm resentful being in this new world that is watching me with keen eyes. A few in the crowd wander away as if I've been one of Mr. Barnum's curious acts and they must hurry to see another. Maybe I can get a job here being the wee Irish girl who entertains the crowd with my recitations. Then I could make a pretty penny!

"Fire away, then," Mr. Whitman says after it quiets down, "but the rest of these fine people might wish to see some other act besides ours." He turns towards the crowd and addresses them. "I'm scheduled to be in the Moral Lecture Room within the hour and you can hear me there. In the meantime, enjoy the other exhibits in this spectacular menagerie of human and animal wonder."

"This is better than a lecture!" shouts someone in the crowd.

"We're happy to watch the child lecture you!" someone else yells.

More laughter rolls around the room and there is a spirit of joviality and cheer, but not within my mind and heart. Not long ago, I thought I might like to meet this Mr. Whitman, but now that it's happening with people listening and watching, I feel like the dog with two legs that is part of an exhibit in the museum.

"We'll ignore them as much as possible," Mr. Whitman says, smiling warmly at me while gesturing towards the crowd. "What would you like to ask of me?"

"Nora, dear," Lavonia interrupts, giving a weak smile to Mr. Whitman, "we are going to look around while you and Mr. Whitman have your conversation. Perhaps we'll catch up with you later."

"Thank you for your kindness," I say to her sweet, but empty face. "I hope you'll have a lovely time."

I pull her sparkling comb out of my hair and hand it to her, aware of eyes in the room looking at my dirty hair that falls in tangles down my back. Lavonia and her friends walk away and I'm relieved to be rid of them, although I should have worked harder at impressing them. Maybe I could have had a decent job working for Lavonia.

I turn towards Mr. Whitman and don't know if I possess the courage to question him about the Irish. I take a deep breath and look at his deeply lined face and into his piercing eyes. "My teacher, Mrs. Drake, reads your poetry in class. Your words make me feel hopeful about this city, which is my new world I'm trying to understand."

"I'm delighted . . . ," he responds, folding his hands together as if in prayer.

"My question is . . ." I hesitate.

"Go ahead . . . go ahead, if you will," he replies, placing his hands behind his back, positioning himself in an observant pose.

"You've written that New York is a '. . . glorious . . . wicked, and magnificent city.' You see, I've memorized some of your words that were printed in the paper. My question is . . . my question is this: Don't you feel this city should welcome the 'coarse, unshaven, and filthy

Irish rabble'? Why do you call us 'Catholic dogs and foreign filth'? Is there no room for us amongst the colors you celebrate in your poetry?"

There! I dared to ask this burning question I had within me! My heart is beating much too fast and my face is flushed. A few cheers erupt from some of the stray onlookers standing near us. I wait for Mr. Whitman to respond, holding my sweaty and shaky hands behind me. For what seems like a long time, we both stand staring at one another with our hands clasped behind our backs. I don't waver from looking at his penetrating eyes because I refuse to be afraid of this American writer!

"I believe it is your religion I take umbrage with, my dear, and not the Irish human flesh that contains the same human heartbeat that beats within us all."

"I thought this country was founded by people who wanted to practice their religion freely. Mrs. Drake taught us this."

"And thus I have the freedom to protest the teaching of Catholic superstition," Mr. Whitman answers.

"I don't understand the religions of the world. I don't understand my own religion very well. If we pray to saints and believe in fairies, you say we're superstitious. We don't believe we're being superstitious. Why should you find fault with us?"

"There are many Irish Catholics attempting to take over parts of this city!"

"You're thinking of the Irish gangs, but not all of us do this. My family and I don't believe in gangs. You need to understand our history in order to understand us. Why have you written about the Irish having committed crimes as Irish men and not just as men? Being from Ireland and being Catholic doesn't make them wicked men. It's being human that gives them the choice to be wicked."

My hands are trembling so fiercely that my whole body begins to shake, too. I'm surprised by these words that have come from somewhere strange within me. Da would be so proud of me for standing up to this Mr. Whitman!

"Well, well . . ." Mr. Whitman grins broadly at me. He doesn't speak for a moment, but continues smiling at me.

"I don't disagree with your insights, my dear child. I am even capable of believing in the chorus of dissonant voices rising to create a symphony. However, I do not believe in one voice prevailing over all others. I fear that there can be too much power wielded by one voice . . . and that voice is in danger of becoming an Irish Catholic voice. I embrace you and your people as part of the landscape of this magnificent city. And tonight, you have enriched my experience in this city just by our conversation. I hope you can transcend the place you have come from and become a vital and beautiful part of this city."

Mr. Whitman releases his hands from behind his back and puts them in prayer position again, still smiling at me. It is clear to me that this American poet is being sincere, as sincere as he can possibly be.

"If you'll please excuse me, I must go to my lecture now," he says while pulling out his pocket watch. Then he bows before me. "I hope we meet again sometime."

"The Lord bless and keep you, Mr. Whitman," I say, smiling with my mouth closed so my teeth don't show. In my grand speech, I had forgotten about them and how tattered my clothing is. Then there is clapping as if we had been part of an interesting performance. I suddenly remember that I was supposed to meet Mam at Mr. Stewart's to interview for a job. I grab my coat and make my way outside feeling disappointed that I won't be able to see the fascinations and marvels of P. T. Barnum's grand museum. People pat me on my back as I go, saying, "well done, wee one."

I'm weary of being called "wee one," but I'm just plain weary from being me sometimes, except I'm excited about the experience I've just had in this strange place. Now I'm standing on a cold street, feeling wretched just like Cinderella when her midnight hour struck and her magic disappeared! How fast my feelings slide down from the glory of my head to my ragged and cold feet! I see flashes of light and hear gunfire going off. I look up and there are lights flashing on and off on top of Barnum's Museum. Is it on fire? Is it being blown to pieces? I wonder. I look right and left and begin running down the street. Then I hear a voice calling my name. I turn around and it's my dear friend, Sean!

Chapter Thirteen

A NEW SEAN

She was a Phantom of delight
When first she gleamed upon my sight;
A lovely Apparition, sent
To be a moment's ornament . . .
—William Wordsworth

"There she is . . . a phantom of delight!" Sean beams at me. He looks different—maybe older and taller . . . and clean. That's it! Sean looks clean because he's groomed and his clothing isn't tattered. And doesn't this make him look the handsome lad, I think, as I huddle on the cold street in my worn out dead girl's coat. More lights explode in the sky above the museum and there are big booms. People are uttering little screams and staring into the sky.

"God with my soul, what is happening?" I ask Sean.

"It's the fireworks show Mr. Barnum gives the city every night." Sean takes my arm. "Let's go for a cup of tea." He is so grown up and sure of himself!

I'm curious where we're going for a cup of tea. We walk away from the museum and I keep looking back at the bursts of light in the sky. Now that I know what it is, I wish we could stay to view the show. I'm sorry that I didn't see much of the museum and now I'm not going to see the fireworks. Sean tells me about his new job working at the docks loading the cargo ships and cleaning passenger ships en route to Europe. As we walk down the street, I remember Mam again! By now, Mam and Meg will be home from work and they'll be wondering what happened to me. I shouldn't be going for tea with Sean.

"I best not be going with you for tea," I say, stopping on the sidewalk. Sean looks at me with disappointment.

"Am I disgusting to you, Nora? Don't you want to be with a real Irish gentleman?"

I giggle because I can't imagine Sean as a gentleman, nor can I imagine any Irishman a gentleman. Not in the sense of what I know about gentlemen, like the ones in the carriage and English gentlemen.

"You're not disgusting, Sean O'Connolly. I'm pleased to be alongside you walking down the street, but I need to get home. I promised Mam I would go to the Stewart Mansion to apply for a job after school, but I never made it. I was carted off by a carriage full of perfumed ladies and pompous gentlemen who were going to the museum. They thought me amusing and I've lost track of time and now I'll be in trouble. But I don't know how to get home from this part of the city," I say, shivering in the cold and looking around the streets wondering which one to take.

"I'd never leave a young lady on a street alone at night. I'll escort you home." Sean takes my arm and leads me down the street. When I tell him about the apartment tumbling and how we moved to another one in Five Points, he leans down and kisses my cheek!

"Why did you do that?" I stop walking and my face reddens as a holly berry.

"Just in case the building you live in now collapses and I never get to touch my lips to your lovely face!"

I almost jump out of my coat and skin because I'm frightened by his affection, but I am also warmed.

"I don't think you should be saying these things, Sean O'Connolly!"

"Sean O'Connolly wouldn't be saying these things, but Sean Connolly, a real American, would."

"Does that mean you won't be going back to Ireland with me if you're now a real American?"

"I'm working at the docks making more money than when I was a newsie. Before you know it, I'll be a captain's mate. My work is grand now, and the ship owners trust me. And then I'll be going back and forth across the sea all the time. We'll be going together to Ireland on one of those trips, to be sure. Maybe we'll have two homes then. One in New York and one in Ireland!"

"I only want my home in Ireland."

"You'd want to be leaving New York? Look at how many jobs I've had here! Anything is possible. I can one day dream and scheme, and the next day, I'm living the dream. Who'd ever thought I'd be a newsie and filling my pockets full of coins. And then to get work on the docks! The possibilities are limitless here, Nora. I can become a fireman, a grocer, a boxer, or even a captain of a ship. Maybe I can even become another John Astor!"

"And don't you miss the green fields and mountains of Ireland? Doesn't your heart ache to see your family and don't you miss the telling of stories around the hearth?"

"I don't miss eating nothing but praties (potatoes) and buttermilk day after day until even they don't exist for us to eat. I don't miss bowing down to the English and wishing we could live in one of their mansions, when here we can work hard enough and get our own mansion."

I've stopped shivering because I'm so mad that my whole body has heated up. I place my hands on my hips and although I'm tired from challenging Mr. Whitman, I'm ready to take on Sean!

"Don't you see how poor people are here? Have you shut your ears to the taunts and remarks we get by the people who call us filthy swine and 'paddy this and paddy that'? How long will it take you to become rich enough to own a mansion? Will you join a gang and bow down to the politicians in this city who will corrupt your soul to the core? My Da says it's so, and it's no different from the secret societies in Ireland who want to murder the English. Do they win? No, they die with blood on their hands and still there's no freedom for our country. I want to go back and climb the green hills and listen to the stories. Even if they are mournful and tragic tales about our land, it's my land. I can dream there, and if the praties rot again in the ground, I will come here to survive and then return again to Ireland. I believe I've left my feet in Ireland, Sean. I haven't really danced since I came to this city. A wee jig here and there only to keep me warm, but it isn't really dancing!

"I planted my foot print in the soil in Cork before we left, but I feel as if I've left my very feet there sometimes. Oh sure, I danced on the ship, but it was the shadow of my feet following me and begging me not to leave or give up my Irish heart. I am sorely disappointed in you, Sean O'Connolly!"

I turn and run down the street, bumping into fancy dressed ladies and drunken old men. I don't care. I hate this city. There are only glimmers of light here that tease me and taunt me into believing there is hope for new life. And when I climbed out of the Cinderella carriage, I found it had turned into a pumpkin and my clothes were still in rags. And the people of this land are mean and insincere. Tears flow down my face, for not only has my Da given up the dream to return to Ireland, Sean has given it up, too. I don't belong here. I can't find any American shoes to fit my feet because I left my feet back in Ireland!

Sean runs after me calling my name. I keep running and the tears I thought I had left behind me on the ship are pouring out of me. I am hungry, tired, and confused. I just want to go home. "I just want to go home!" I whimper as I run.

"Nora, I'm sorry! Don't run away from me!" Sean yells, and when he reaches me, I stop running. He takes my hands in his and looks straight into my eyes.

"As soon as I can, I'll go to Ireland with you. I can't promise I'll stay there long but I'll go with you. And when I leave to come back here, I'll go again to see you if you are still there. Dry up your tears, wee one."

I cuff Sean playfully on the side of the head and begin giggling.

"What was that for?"

"For calling me 'wee one,' Sean O'Connolly!"

"I'll not call you 'wee one' if you promise to call me 'Sean Connolly.'"

"I can't promise that. You were born with an 'O' and in my eyes, you'll always have an 'O.'"

Chapter Fourteen

STEPPING OUT WITH SEAN

Believe me, if all those endearing young charms,
Which I gaze on so fondly today, Were to change
by tomorrow, and fleet in my arms, Like
faery-gifts fading away, Thou wouldst still
be adored, as this moment thou art . . .
— Thomas Moore

When Sean and I arrive at my apartment, there's a note from Mam. She and Meg are at a neighbor's having tea and they want me to immediately join them when I return. She doesn't mention being angry at me for not showing up at the Stewart Mansion as planned. I'm relieved, but Mam is hard to figure out these days and I never know when she'll be angry or easy going towards me and my behavior. I decide to have tea with Sean rather than go to an old neighbor's for a dull evening. I scribble out a note saying I have gone with Mary to a play and I'll be home soon. I'll have to pray for forgiveness for lying, but I don't think Mam would like me to be out with Sean having tea.

Sean waits for me in the hallway as I wash my face and hands with the water from the tub in the kitchen. I am embarrassed to be covered with city grime from being out all day. I brush my hair and pinch my cheeks for color, although the cold winter air has already given them ample rosyness. *Godey's Lady's Book* instructs young women to pinch their cheeks to obtain a healthy blush to make them more attractive. I wish I had some toilet water to dab on my neck like *Godey's* instructs young women, but I've never even smelled any. I ignore the grumbling in my stomach and the tiredness I feel as I prepare for another adventure—stepping out for evening tea with Sean! I make the sign of the cross and utter a prayer to God and his fairies for forgiveness and protection.

When we descend the steps of our tenement building, Sean takes my arm as if I am a real lady. It feels wonderful pretending to be a grown woman like I read about in the magazines. I hope he has noticed I've cleaned up a bit, even if I don't have any sweet smelling perfume to wear. I feel safe with Sean, but I'm a wee bit frightened of the change in him that caused him to kiss me on the cheek. I am not ignorant of the dangers of this city and the lurid stares of drunken men. I've heard about what they can do to you in the alleys, and Mam and Meg are always warning me about them. I pull away a little from Sean's arm in mine, just so I'm not too close to him. I look up at him as he looks ahead at where we are going and feel confident that he'd never harm me the way some men might harm women.

"I'd say it was quiet in there for disobeying your Mam," Sean says as we amble down the street.

"No one's home. They're having tea at a neighbor's and I left a note saying I've gone out with Mary." I giggle with excitement, but Sean shakes his head in disapproval.

"It's wrong to lie. I thought you had high principles, Nora."

Shame rushes into my chest like fire, but I put it out by changing the subject.

"And where might we be going on this fine evening as snow drops icy feathers on our heads?" I ask.

"I'm taking the lady out for a night of dancing and revelry!"

I pull away from Sean and stand in front of him, trying to understand the yes and no's, ups and downs, and good and bad I now see coming from him. He isn't the straightforward boy I met a few months ago.

"And who is lying now? You told me we were going for tea. Where are your high principles, Mr. O'Connolly?" I am both frightened and excited by the prospect of dancing. Revelry is another matter and I gaze at him questioningly. Is he just fooling with me?

Sean laughs and places his hands on my shoulders. I don't know if he is serious or not.

"Ye must trust me. I'll not take you anywhere dangerous." He takes my arm again and we walk down the street.

My heart is beating faster and faster as we walk. Women don't go to saloons and are known only to purchase the pints and drink them at the grocer's, but children are certainly not allowed into a saloon. I never heard of dancing around here except in the saloons.

"'Tis a special place underneath the city for fairies of all colors and ages," Sean says as he squeezes my arm and laughs loudly. I pull on his arm and look up at him. He winks at me and I wonder if he really believes in fairies.

"Then I will certainly be at home there," I say.

As we walk, the snow falls heavier and the wind throws the cold flakes upon us. It is very dark, but there are still vendors selling oysters and hot chestnuts. Sean stops to buy some chestnuts and says that we'll save them to eat later. They'll be cold then, I want to say, but I don't. My stomach grumbles and I don't know if I can wait until later to eat them. A few minutes later, he stops at a storefront shop that is still open. There are boots and colorful woolen scarves hanging under an awning. He picks out a blue scarf and we go into the shop to pay for it. I am happy to be inside and out of the cold for a few minutes while he makes his purchase. I think he's going to wrap it around my neck and I'll be mighty grateful, but why isn't he saving his money—sending it back home to his family in Ireland or saving it for our trip back to Ireland? When we're outside again, he takes the beautiful royal blue scarf and wraps it around my neck.

"This is for a queen. Maybe you're a descendant of Queen Maeve or better yet, a fairy queen. I don't know, wee one, but you're royalty to me. A royal heart you carry that beats out lines of poetry in the flutter of your eyes. You're a rare one, to be sure."

"And why are you buying such an expensive gift for me, O'Connolly? You must be saving your coins for our trip back to Ireland."

I only want to talk about practical matters because these things he's saying are just not true and I don't know this new Sean O'Connolly. Maybe it's true—he is Sean Connolly, missing his O, the American boy now, not the Irish lad I thought I knew.

"We'll be taking no trips to Ireland in the winter where we'll run into icebergs. By the time spring comes, my coins will be bursting in the seams of me pants. Then we can go to Ireland."

I am warmed by the scarf, for the soft warmth of the cloth, but also from the giver's affection towards me.

Chapter Fifteen

NORA FINDS HER DANCING FEET

We foot it all the night.
Weaving olden dances.
Mingling hands and mingling glances
Til the moon has taken flight . . .
—W. B. Yeats, "The Stolen Child"

I am no longer cold by the time we reach our des-
tination. The new scarf has wrapped warm blue magic
around me. I feel as light as a cloud floating in the sky
on a summer day, although it is the dead of a winter
night. My old companion, fear, who sometimes walks
behind me, before me, or at my side, has disappeared
for the time being. Sean and I have walked to Anthony
Street, which is between Centre and Orange Streets. I
have walked this way many times to sell newspapers.
People are thronging the street, smoking, laughing,
and singing, even in the bitter cold air. A few children
lean their heads back and stick out their tongues to
catch the miniature white flakes that are falling down
upon us. I glance at the faces surrounding me and see
bright and hopeful eyes on faces molded in all sorts of
shapes and sizes. The snow has made us all clean and
the stars have fallen from the sky into our eyes. The
poverty that is amongst us on this city street hides in
the background this night as joy and celebration take

center stage. I stand frozen in the moment before Sean takes my hand and leads me through the door of a large brick building and down two flights of stairs to the basement. As we carefully make our way down the steps that are thronging with jubilant people, I hear music. It is lively and exuberant music that makes my heart almost burst through my body. I haven't heard this music since I set my feet, my new American feet, upon the soil of this country. Sean squeezes my hand as we enter a room that is smoky, dimly lit, but filled with music of my former heart. This is music that possesses ancient rhythms, and as it fills me when I walk into its presence, I see my Da sitting in a corner next to a very dark-skinned man! Hands, fingers, arms, fiddles and bows all move in unison that is fast and full of joy that is heavenly. Da is playing his fiddle again! I'm so happy for him, but puzzled and hurt that he has kept this place secret from us and has not invited us here. I walk towards him, but he doesn't look up and I decide to not interrupt him because I don't want these moments of ecstasy in this strange place to disappear. I stare at him, but he sees nothing but his own fingers on his fiddle. It is Irish music, our music, but with strange and mysterious new sounds that coat and thicken what is familiar to my ears. It is as if our music has put on new jewels for a night on the town!

"Soon there'll be dancing!" Sean has come up behind me and shouts in my ear. He doesn't know my Da is contributing to these glorious sounds. He takes my hand and leads me to the side of the room that has a row of chairs up against the wall. We sit on two empty chairs and my whole being takes in my surroundings with elation and expectation.

There is a clean and sanded floor, whitewashed walls and ceiling, from which hangs a large chandelier full of burning candles. The room is small and large at the same time, filled to capacity with people, but the ceiling high enough for the chandelier. I am at home with the music, but what is most surprising is that there is a mix of black-skinned people and white-skinned people gathering together to dance on the dance floor in the middle of the room.

"This is Pete Williams Dance Hall," Sean shouts in my ear. "It's owned by a black man. He's a very rich bachelor and owns a team of race horses. It's clean and cheerful all right, but it does have a bad reputation." He winks at me and smiles.

I don't care if it has a bad reputation, for I'm thrilled to be here! There is no fear at all to be in such a place as this! If my Da plays his music here and Sean has brought me here, it is a grand place to be! My mind flits back to the time at the museum and I think of Mr. Whitman and his poetry. Does he know about this? Well then, if he prefers lectures to dancing, I am sorry for his troubles!

The dancing begins as each gentleman flings his arms around his partner and gives a quick and light kiss on her cheek. Those around me who are watching begin whooping and clapping to the music as the dancers stand in lines dancing jigs and reels. I can hardly hold still, but I put my hands together and clap. My body begins moving all over the chair and Sean is clapping and laughing at me. The dancers dance alone and with their partners, as well as in configurations with other couples. A black man picks up a tambourine and hits it against his head, heels, knees, and elbows to the music. The dancers become more and more aroused as the musicians quicken the tempo. Eventually it seems all figures are forgotten and the dancers become so wild with excitement that they leap frantically about, clasping their partners in their arms.

Da has not once looked up from his fingers, but the pints keep coming his way. He keeps his head down and I wonder if he's ashamed to be in this place, for he has said the saloons in New York are no place for the

McCabes. Then I should feel shame to be in a place where bodies are gyrating, sweating, and there is kissing and closeness, but I don't. I am home here because there is the music of home. It has taken on new tones and expressions, but it is my music, our music, and it means that we have a place here in America. We're the despised paddies and filthy swine! Let there be fancy carriages, lecture halls, and opera houses in this city. I want this! I want the music of home that will help me remember my feet I've left behind in Cork City. My dancing feet! The music stops, but only for a minute. My Da never looks up, but begins playing again, the other musicians following him in the tune. It is a familiar tune to me, one I've nearly forgotten. It is a lilting hornpipe that calls for constrained and precise steps that the visiting dance masters used to teach us when they visited our villages in Ireland. I don't know if I can remember the steps, but I can no longer sit in my chair and hold my body still. People are moving freestyle to the music, but no one is dancing to the hornpipe. The tambourine player isn't playing, the other musicians struggle to play with Da and stop altogether. Now it is only my Da playing, his long and crooked fingers holding the bow. The smoky room filled with the noisy crowds hushes to listen and it is then I know that I must dance this hornpipe and find my feet again, my own Irish dancing feet.

I'm wearing old leather black boots, laced up with some twine that I found in the market one day. There's a two-inch heel on them that gives me some height, and although I am called "wee one," I feel much taller wearing the boots. They are the perfect size for me now, and I have a feeling they'll be good partners for my feet on the dance floor. I whisper to Sean that I'll be returning soon and then I jump up, tap my toes on the floor and try out the heels with a few taps. I take off my dirty coat, check to see if the buttons are all secured on my dress, run my fingers through my tangled hair, and tie my new scarf around my neck so it will not be lost. I need it for bravery. And then I whisper to the fairies, "As free as you all are dancing on the wind and riding snowflakes to the earth, visit my feet tonight and make them sing!" Then I am almost lifted and carried into the middle of the room, and when I am there, the people step back and look at me as if they instinctively know I'm about to perform. For a moment, all I can hear is my heart beating loudly and rapidly in my chest and ears, but then it takes on a new rhythm in time with the music being played. I take a moment to let it regulate to that particular rhythm, the rhythm of my Da's fingers on the fiddle and the rhythm of the hornpipe. I wait for this beat to fill my body and burn into my feet so that I can dance.

I begin dancing and I find that my feet have memory. I lift my legs and tap out the steps to this graceful dance, a dance my mind had hidden away when I was deep in the hold of the ship. The smoke in the room swirls around me like clouds and I shut my eyes and only hear the music of my heart, the music of my Da, the music of my Ireland. I forget time and place, and I am suddenly thousands of memories old . . . as old as the ancient stones, fairies, and stories from Ireland. The music and my feet have brought me home again. I am home again and I haven't gone back across the sea. And when the music stops, I open my eyes and look into my Da's eyes, eyes much like my own. He smiles at me and I know there is hope in this city of New York.

Chapter Sixteen

An Eatery

. . . all is moving and removing, organizing and
disorganizing, building up and tearing down; the
ever active spirit of change seems to pervade all
things, and all places in this mighty metropolis.
—J. C. Myers

I walk over to my Da and the people around me
clap and shout praise.

"*A storin*, you are here?" Da asks me, a soft happiness of surprise on his face. I'm relieved he isn't angry
at me for being in the saloon.

"I've danced, Da! I've danced a hornpipe in
America!"

"Is your Mam here? Who is with you?" Da asks as
his eyes glide over the room.

"Mam isn't here. It's just me and Sean."

"Have I met the lad?" Da stands up, setting his
fiddle to rest on the side of his chair. The other musicians nod and smile at me and I smile back at them.

"I don't know. I'll bring him over."

I walk through the crowd to find Sean standing
next to his chair talking to some people. I motion for
him to follow me and when we're standing in front of
Da, I make introductions. Sean shakes Da's hand and
Da stares seriously into his face.

"And what are you doing with my daughter, lad?" he asks.

"I'm protecting her from the streets of New York and treating her like a lady," Sean replies. He puts his shoulders back and puffs up his chest.

"Where's your family from?" Da asks, looking Sean up and down, sizing him up.

"Clare, sir. Clare, we're from . . ."

"You'd best be taking her home now to her Mam," Da interrupts. "It's late and she'll be worrying."

"Yes, sir, I'll get her home safe and sound." Sean shakes Da's hand again. "Grand fiddling, Mr. McCabe, grand fiddling altogether!" Sean is smiling at Da as he takes my arm to leave.

I pull away from Sean. "But Da, I want to do some more dancing. You never told us you were coming to this place! How come you've kept it a secret?"

"Go on home now, Nora. 'Tis no place for my daughter."

People in the crowd yell for more music and the musicians ask Da to play with them again. Sean takes my arm and as we make our way back to our chairs to retrieve our coats, I am overcome with exhaustion and hunger. I had supernatural strength to dance, but now there is nothing left in me. It had to be the touch of the fairies that made my legs fly! People speak to me as we try to make our way outside the building. Some of the black women are asking me to teach them the dance I just did and I promise them I'll come back, but I know Da will never allow me to return here because it is a rough place. There are couples locked together in tight embraces in the corners of the room and men and women staggering from drinking too many pints. Da will never let me come back to dance here, I think sadly, just when I have found some of Ireland here to hold me up until I return. I promise myself that I must find a way to dance in New York!

"I'm hungry, Sean O'Connolly," I say to him when we are outside the building. "When do we eat the chestnuts that are now cold in your pocket?"

"I forgot all about the chestnuts. Saints be praised, the hunger left me watching you dance!"

"You best not be fresh, O'Connolly!" I say.

We walk down the street and away from the building that hides my Irish world in it, another world within worlds. I'm reluctant to walk away from it and I nearly turn back. Da is still there in this world, a world he went to without us, and soon he'll be going to another world in California! I stop walking and put my hands over my face. A sob is stuck inside my chest and I don't want it to rise to my eyes. I push on my eyes with my fingers so the tears won't come.

"'Tis no need to cry, Nora. Ye're a lovely dancer . . ."

"I'm not crying! I'm hungry, Sean, I'm just very hungry at the moment."

Sean doesn't understand what I'm feeling and I'm not going to tell him either. I press on my eyelids a little more and feel the tears course their way back down to my chest. I lift my head and pound on my chest a bit to get myself together.

"Let's get something to eat, then," he says, and we walk down the street again.

When we reach a corner, Sean stops and pulls out a cigar from his pocket. He lights it, blows pungent smoke into the icy air, and coughs.

"And what are you doing smoking like an old Irish woman, O'Connolly?" I ask as I hit him on the back.

"It's an American . . . an American cigar, and an expensive one. I've saved it and now I'm enjoying it with my lady."

"I'm not your lady . . . but I am a lady and I'm asking you to put out that horrid smellin' cigar right this minute!"

Sean immediately extinguishes the cigar in the snow and puts it into his pocket. He takes my arm and walks me into a very small diner. Over the top of the diner, I notice it says, "Eats." I wonder why they couldn't have come up with a more interesting name, but I'm pleased to be taken into one of these establishments. I've only been inside a bakery and the grocer's, but never an eatery. I'm nervous, but Sean guides me inside and sits us down at a tiny table in the corner by the window. We look out into the street and watch the people wander by, most of them miserable looking, but tonight as the snowflakes fall upon them under the softness of gaslights, they transform into story book characters before my eyes.

"We'll have the blue plate special," Sean tells the man who comes to take our order.

"For two?" he asks, and then hesitates after Sean nods yes.

"You got money, right?"

"Would I be in here ordering if I didn't?" Sean answers, his face growing red and anger searing his words.

"No need to get yourself in a huff, boy," the man answers as he walks away to put in our order.

Sean pounds his fist on the table. "Who does he think he is!" he whispers.

"What is a blue plate special?" I ask.

"Hots and beans . . . hots and beans. Now that I'm a dock worker, I should be eating steak, but I've got a right taste for this kind of food."

"What are hots?"

"Hot dogs! You don't know about hot dogs?"

I feel slightly sick. How could Americans eat dogs? I thought Americans were a bit fussy about their eating, but some of them must be as desperate as the Irish were during the Famine.

"I'm not eating any dogs, Sean O'Connolly. I'm leaving right now. I'm tired from a whole day of strange things happening to me. Strange people in a fancy carriage, Mr. Walt Whitman himself talking to me, and then I find Da drinking pints and playing fiddle down in the basement of an old building. I find my dancing feet and learn that Ireland is here in America, too, but no matter how hungry I am, I won't eat a dog! Even if it's an American dog!"

I stand up to leave, but Sean pulls me down next to him. When I plunk down and turn to him, he kisses me on the cheek.

"Do ya think kisses will keep me here to eat this horror?" I say as I begin to get up again.

"No, but I need to keep both sides of your face even with a kiss, otherwise, one side will be pining for a kiss, too!"

I gently slap Sean on the side of his face. "There now, turn the other cheek and I'll slap that one, too. You're being much too fresh!"

"We're not really going to eat a dog," Sean says, beginning to laugh so hard that he has to hold his stomach.

"Maybe not a real dog running the streets, but a dead one, I'm sure," I answer.

"There's no dog!" Sean laughs, unable to speak. I get up and sit down on the opposite side of the table from him.

"It's a kind of meat . . . pork, you know . . . pig . . . ," he says when he gets himself under control.

"Pig . . . dog . . . whatever is running on some legs and can be slaughtered to feed us poor people," I say, disgusted, but my stomach still grumbles and begs for food.

"You've had the sausages at home, Nora. Hot dogs are sort of like the sausages."

Just then, two plates of steaming food arrive at our table. The man sets down some spoons and mugs of coffee, too. I look down and see a pool of tiny little brown beans and floating in them are the funniest look-ing dogs I've ever seen.

"You didn't say we'd be eating just the tail, Sean O'Connolly!"

Chapter Seventeen

LOVELY SNOW

> I remembered the gradual patience
> That fell from that cloud like snow,
> Flake by flake, healing and hiding
> The scar that renewed our woe . . .
> —James Russell Lowell

New York has adorned itself in diamond snow crystals as if it is preparing for a grand ball. The snow drapes over each one of us when we walk outside, whether we are wearing tattered rags or rich tapestry and finery. We are made clean and new as we stroll or rush through the streets together. We walk amongst one another as one people this winter because we are adorned in white by the merciful sky. It isn't as cold as my first winter in America and I am actually falling in love with snow. It falls in a slow dance and waltzes its way into my heart. I lift my face and welcome its refreshing touch. I close my eyes and imagine that each flake is the touch of angel wings, so gentle even in its shocking cold. Sometimes early in the morning, I go into an alley that is filled with snow untouched by human feet. Mrs. Drake has shown us how to make angels in the snow. I lie down in its freshly fallen soft blankets and close my eyes, moving my arms and legs back and forth as if in a dance. And then I try to get up and stand in the imprint and jump as far away as possible from the angel I have made. I believe that this angel isn't really made by me, but is real and lives close behind me to guide me. It imprints onto the snow when I lie down and will surely get up to be with me again as I walk away. I see fairies creating sparkles around the outside of the imprint as the sun shines through cracks between buildings, beaming their way onto my snow angel.

Sean, Mary, and I ice-skate on a pond outside Five Points, although we don't have real skates. Our shoes are slippery enough and we don't mind not having skates, although we have to skate when there aren't many others with real ice skates. We heard a story about a little boy's finger being sliced off by another skater with sharp blades when he fell down.

Sean is making good money working on the docks preparing passenger ships for travel in spring. He bought Mary and me mittens to warm our hands and fingers. I have never had a pair of mittens and love the way I can curl up my fingers inside them to keep extra warm on a cold day. They are royal blue, like my scarf, the color I know queens must wear. We keep our bellies filled and warmed with hot chestnuts and hot chickpeas that are sold and served in newspapers shaped like cones. These cones are called "toots" and all three of us, being former newsies, wish we had thought of this innovative way to use the leftover newspapers we never sold. We could have sold them to food vendors to sell their food in on the streets.

I'm still planning and saving to go to Ireland in the springtime. Although I have fallen in love with snow in New York and have found my dancing feet again, I talk to my friends about returning to Ireland. It's a fierce and powerful feeling I have in the deep well of me that makes me hunger to return. Home. I need the place that is home. The home I remember that is in Ireland. I'm worried about Da and his private meetings he goes to when he isn't playing his fiddle at the saloon. One night, Sean and I returned to the dance hall, but Da didn't see us come in. We moved about secretly watching Da, and during a break, we heard him talking about his plans to go to California. He said that he's going with one of the B'Hoys! We can't believe that Da is aligning himself with this group, most of them being the American-born Irish ones who think they're better than those of us born in Ireland. Why is Da making friends with such men! These men use coercion and violence to get what they want from city officials. I asked Mam, but she told me to mind my own business! Things have gotten worse between the members of our family. I wonder if we are even a family anymore! Mam used to give me an occasional kiss atop my head, but she lectures me now and her voice is harsh, as are her words. She said I'm not acting like I should for a young Irish girl.

"Nora, I think you're in danger of putting on airs since we've moved to this city," Mam said the night I asked about Da. "You've become the uppity one, too, refusing to work with me at the Stewart Mansion and coming and going when you please. You'll not be questioning me about your Da!"

Mam walked away and looked out the window, folding her arms tightly in front of her. I could clearly see tears falling down her cheeks. She doesn't see my Da that much herself, but she's always the strong and proud one.

Although I'm not working with Mam at Stewart's, I'm bringing home money for my family and keep the rest with what I've already saved in my dresser. I'm working with Mary at her friend's apartment making flowers to sell to milliners. These flowers are sewed onto expensive ladies' hats and bring us good pay, as long as we produce a lot of them. We work three days a week after school and all day on Saturday. I like working with my hands and I also want to purchase one of these fine and fancy hats one day. I've promised myself that I will buy one in the spring and return to Ireland in style.

"Mary," I said to her one day, "what if I go to Ireland and then Mam, Da, and Meg won't return? What if something happens to my dresser? What if the starving is still going on and my money runs out and I can't get back here and never see my dresser and family again?"

"What if . . . what if . . . my Nora, ye are the troubled one all right. 'What ifs' never do anyone any good. You need to have more faith, wee one."

"Not you, too! Don't be calling me wee one or you'll be without a best friend!"

"And who said you're my best friend?" she said, giggling.

"You did! And you know I am!" I said as I started to run away from her.

"Last one to the corner is a rotten egg!" I yell, and the two of us sprint down the street dodging people, some of them yelling at us and calling us ill mannered children.

I've had a long day and my fingers are stiff from making flowers and also from the chilly apartment. I'm wearing my mittens as I lie down next to the dresser to nap until Da returns home. I'm nearly sleeping when he comes home, trying to be quiet so as not to wake us. He probably smells like the pints he's been drinking and he'll be in another world far from us, but he's still my Da and I desperately need to talk to him. I've been having dreams of being on the ship without my dresser, lying on a bunk with two old men who have no teeth and who smell like cow dung. Last night I dreamed that someone threw my dresser overboard into the tossing sea!

"Is that you, *a storin?*" Da asks when I begin to move towards him in the dark room.

"It's me, Da. Can I light a candle? I need to talk to you."

"Have you been going to Mass and making your confessions, Nora?"

"Da, I'm serious. I'm in a bad way to talk to you tonight."

"Light the candle and we'll sit at the table." Da stumbles in the dark and I hear him pull out a chair. I feel for the match lying near the candle on the table and strike it. As I light the candle, I look into Da's unshaven and sorrowful face. His hair is long and needs a cut; he looks weary, wearier than ever I've seen him in America. He puts his elbows on the table and rests his head in his hands.

"A cup of tea would be grand, Nora. Is there any way . . ."

"I've prepared the tea, Da."

After Mam and Meg were sound asleep, I prepared the tea and kept water simmering for this time together. I'm pleased with myself for having timed it just right. I pour water into the teapot and cover it with the tea cozy for it to steep. I bring it and the mug over to the table.

"Is the milk frozen on the window sill?" Da asks.

"No more milk, Da. We ran out after we had our tea this evening, but I'll buy some at the grocer's tomorrow."

"This is lovely, Nora. Lovely altogether to be here late at night sipping tea with my daughter."

I let Da relax and sip his tea. Although I smell the pints and smoke on him, he isn't drunk. I've never seen my Da drunk, here in America or at home in Ireland. I don't want to burden him too much because he has to get up early to work at the bank cleaning it before customers and employees come in. Then he has to clean up the street in front of the bank, too. Da has never lost his dignity doing this kind of work, but I know he's weary, especially having to work in the snow and cold. If only he could make enough money playing his fiddle because it's the only thing that brings back the life into his old bones.

"What might it be that is troubling ye, my Nora?" he asks.

"I want to know about your trip to California . . ."

Da takes a deep breath and looks up at the dark ceiling. "Don't go getting any notions in that wee head of yours. It's not fit for children of any age, especially a girl, to go on the long journey to Californie."

"But I want to know that you'll be safe and returning soon. Do you remember how long I waited for you to come home from working on the roads in Ireland?"

Da looks at me in the candlelight and sighs heavily. "On my soul, Nora, I can't believe I'm sitting here now after living through it. I'll never forget it. The saints be praised. I'll never forget."

"Are you glad we're here? Is America grand, Da?"

Da puts his disheveled head back down on his hands. He doesn't say anything for a minute.

With his head in his hands, he says, "America is grand all right . . . It's so grand that it'd like to ship us all back to the ole country. It's so grand that the only way a man can get a decent job is by dirty politics . . ."

"But Da, we aren't starving as we were. We have food here, even though there's never a grand feast or anything like a Cake party. It's been good for us to be here, Da, but not forever. The family back home is writing us that things are better now in Ireland. Soon we'll be able to go home. Right, Da? Cousin Michael says our home hasn't been torn down and it's there waiting for us. He stays there sometimes to take care of it. We have a little land there, too. A few acres are much more than we have here. And this isn't our own home . . ."

"Hold your tongue, Nora!" Da slams a fist down on the table and I'm fearful he'll wake Mam and Meg.

"Someday, God willing, we'll go back. Someday . . . but not now!" His eyes have fire in them as he looks at me.

"You're still a child and you have no understanding! Even though the Famine isn't as terrible as it was when we left, death is still stalking the land. And the British are rallying on against us. It's no time now to be returning. Why are you so keen on going back? Aren't you pleased with school and eating some fine food here? Isn't it grand running through the streets and making friends here? We're all together and isn't it a miracle . . ."

Da stops in mid-sentence and a whimper comes out of him. He puts his head in his hands again. He must be remembering our Kate who is no longer with us. He forgot and said that we were all together, but we're not all together! He gets up, stretches and yawns. I don't want him to go to bed yet, not until I ask him about the B'Hoys.

"It's time we sleep. I'm tired and old, Nora . . ."

"Da . . . I need to ask you one more question . . ."

He sighs again, but sits down and looks at me. I know he's trying to ready himself for another question he doesn't want to answer.

"Just one more, but I won't promise I'll answer it. And then ye must go to sleep."

"What about the B'Hoys? Are you going with them to California? How can you trust them? Most of them hate us and resent us being here. They're roughs, Da. They fight with brick bats and control many of the people in Five Points. You won't be safe going to California with the lot of them."

"Why are ye half the old woman and half the child, Nora? You need to stay the child now and trust your parents to do right by you. You're thinking beyond your years."

"I was a child. I was a child who was left on the ship alone to come to this strange city. But now I'm no longer a child. I've gone through too much to still be a child who feels safe and protected. I know about hunger and death. I know the terrible killing that goes on. I know about the hookers . . ."

"Hookers? Where did ye ever get such a name? What do you know about them? The prostitutes? The call girls? You know of them, wee one?" Da has stood up again and is angry. I know he isn't really angry at me, but is angry he can't keep me a child and keep me safe.

"It's too late, Da . . . too late to go back to my child's place in our family. I'm old enough to make my own money and old enough to go back home to Ireland. I want to go back, and if I do, I can have everything ready for you and Mam to come later on."

"Nora, ye are the strange one. That you are . . . don't go getting notions in your head about going back. Wait until I come home from California. Then we'll see about returning to the ole country. Let's sleep now. Tomorrow comes early enough."

Da kisses the top of my head and I lie down next to the dresser feeling the weight of what I must do. I am going to Ireland in the spring, with or without Da, Mam, Meg, Sean, or Mary.

Chapter Eighteen

THEATER MAGIC

All the world's a stage, And all men
and women merely players . . .
—Shakespeare

This New York winter must be designed by God
and his fairies to woo me into celebrating snow and
city life! Although I'm sad that my family is going in
separate ways and we are rarely home together, I watch
a pattern of joy and surprise weaving its designs in
this strange and magical city. Is it my royal blue scarf
and mittens that keep me warm when the sparkling
snow falls cold upon me? Is it Sean's hand holding mine
inside of my mitten as we stroll down the streets and
eat warm chestnuts? Is it Mary's adventurous spirit
united with mine that brings us laughter and excitement? Maybe it's the city itself, with its unique heartbeat coursing its way through each of us, whether we
are native or foreign born. Ancient songs don't live
deep in the earth in New York City the way they do in
Ireland, but there are ancient songs from Ireland, Africa, and from around the world filling the streets with
a new song of hope and celebration. They don't reso-
nate from deep within the land where our feet trod,
but they vibrate in the air as we all crowd together on
the streets and in the dance halls. I thought the fairies

only lived in the hills, glens, and lakes, but I've been
learning different. They have found beauty in a city,
too, and they are opening my eyes to it.

I have also fallen in love with the theater! I never
knew I'd enjoy Mr. Shakespeare as much as I do, being
that he was an Englishman. He was brilliant! My family
doesn't know about me going to the Bowery Theater
with Sean and Mary. I don't think they'd mind, although
the newspapers say it is one of the wickedest places
under heaven. Many bootblacks and newsies go there
and Sean gets special priced tickets because he was a
newsie for a long time. I don't like the B'Hoys, but I
laugh myself silly when I see a play about one saunter-
ing around the stage in his soap locks, brogue, and
knee breeches wooing an Irish peasant girl. There's a
lot of cursing, yelling, singing, spitting, and throwing
chicken bones during the play, but there is great fun,
too. These plays make us laugh at ourselves and the
self important ones of the city. I don't like it when an
actor pokes fun at an Irishman and portrays him as a
fighting, ignorant, and drunken buffoon. Sure, there
are plenty of them running around the streets of New
York, but not all Irishmen are this way. My Da and Sean
aren't like these Irish characters I watch on stage.

I'm on my way to see Edwin Forrest and Junius
Brutus Booth perform Shakespeare. It is Saturday
evening and Mary and I have worked all day making
flowers. Mam and Meg are visiting with the neighbors
and Da is playing at the dance hall. Mam and Meg have
learned that Da is bringing home extra money working at the dance hall playing music with other musicians. They never go to see him, but they're happy he
is playing his fiddle again, even if it isn't around the
hearth. What hearth? A coal stove is what we have to
keep warm by, and what a dirty mess it is!

I'm feeling grand tonight, because I've gotten
permission from my family to see a Shakespeare play

with Mary and Sean! I didn't tell them it was at the Bowery Theater, but they didn't ask where it was. Maybe they think it's at the Broadway Theater, but I haven't been there yet. It doesn't have the terrible reputation that the Bowery Theater has, and lately there's been talk about people going there to boo an English actor named Macready.

"Move your arse off the street unless ye want to get clubbed like a dog!" yells a boy when I accidentally bump into him. I was looking up into the sky to watch the snowflakes fall for just a moment and ran right into this one. There are about ten boys with him and they're carrying brick bats and on their way to do some kind of evil! I know better than to be in a gang's way, as they are ruthless and pumped up to do violence. Da says they remind him of the stories of the ancient Celts who, on their way to battle, go into a warp-spasm in order to fight. A warp-spasm is a state of becoming pumped up and animal-like, making your blood flow into your muscles. I quickly move out of the way and one of the gang members spits towards me. I jump in time to miss being hit by his angry spewing. I run down the street, hoping this incident doesn't ruin the good feelings I have about the evening at the theater.

I'm breathless from running and from excitement when I arrive in front of the Bowery Theater. There's a crowd waiting to get in and I look around for Sean and Mary. I don't see them at first, but then see them waving at me while they walk across the street.

"We're not going to the Bowery tonight," Mary says, as she takes my arm and moves me away. Sean comes alongside us as Mary scurries me back across the street, dodging carriages and horses.

"We're going to the Chatham Theater a few blocks away," Sean says.

"Why?" I ask, my disappointment growing. "I'm so excited to see a Shakespeare play tonight. The Chatham tickets are dear, aren't they, Sean?"

"No need to worry about that, Nora, I've already bought the tickets."

"Next we'll be going to a ball, Sean O'Connolly!" I say, pleased to be going to a theater more upscale than the Bowery Theater. We walk a few blocks south of the Bowery Theater and find ourselves in front of the Chatham with people waiting to get in.

"I've got news," Sean says. "There's going to be a Five Points Theater some of the newsboys are starting up. It's going to be in a basement in one of the buildings in our neighborhood. I'll be trying out, to be sure, and you ought to consider it although I think it might be a bit too bawdy for the likes of you two." He laughs, shaking his head while looking at us dressed in our fancy clothes. Fancy, but not too fancy, for we can't afford too fancy!

"I've been reciting poems in front of Mrs. Drake's class," I tell my friends. "Isn't that a little like acting?"

"But you don't have to let your bosom hang half out of your dress in front of the class," Mary says, laughing.

"What bosom, Mary?" I whisper into her ear. I didn't want Sean to hear me.

"When will this new theater be opening?" I ask Sean.

"Sometime in spring, but we're recruiting people and saving up money for props and things now."

"Spring is when we go to Ireland."

"I've been meaning to tell you, Nora. I don't know if I'll have enough money," Mary says. "What if the orphanage doesn't let me back in when I come back? I'm already getting too old to be living there, but they don't want to put me out on the streets."

Mary and Sean had both agreed to travel with me to Ireland in the spring, but all along, I suspected they were being too enticed by New York. I will not be kept from going, no matter how much I like New York now!

"Don't you have a cousin in Dublin?" I ask her.

"I have some cousins and old aunts, but they're too poor to help me."

"I'll get you both over there safely," Sean says, "but you won't be going to any plays, eatin' hot chestnuts and skating in winter, or going to the eateries, Nora McCabe."

"I don't care. I'll come back here again when I'm older. I know Mam and Da will go back to Ireland if I'm there. I just know it. And I want our life back as a family. I want a real home." These thoughts badger me and try to ruin my eagerness to see a new play in a new theater with my friends.

"Don't you think you'll be marrying someday and then you won't be living with your family? Wouldn't you like to be here living in a mansion and going to the fancy balls and riding around in carriages with your husband?" Mary asks.

"I won't be marrying anyone. And if I ride around in a carriage, it will be in Ireland and maybe Paris. Then when I'm back in New York I'll have my own carriage."

"My, aren't you the girl with some high falutin' dreams!" Sean says.

"You have your own dreams, Sean O'Connolly, and I can, too!"

"Look, they've opened the doors!" Mary says, jumping up and down. She suddenly hugs Sean's arm. "You're the best friend anyone could have, Sean!" she says.

I turn away and pretend not to notice Mary's show of affection towards Sean. First of all, I thought I was Mary's best friend and I didn't know she felt so close to Sean. Secondly, it looks to me she's being a bit too forward grabbing his arm like that. Something is welling up inside and crawling right up into my cheeks making them heated, and it's not the blushing I do now and then, either. My head is throbbing and I feel as if I'm going to cry. What is wrong with me now? I wonder. By the time we walk through the doors of the theater, I've figured it out. I'm jealous of Mary's friendship with Sean. I have taken it for granted that I am Sean's special friend and never considered that anyone else, like another girl, could be special to him, too. Oh, this night seems to be going all wrong. I hardly notice the lights and décor of the Chatham Theater because I'm so upset with Mary, with Sean, but mostly, with myself.

We sit in the balcony and look down on a stage that has only a few props. A band is playing loudly and out of tune. I manage to sit between Sean and Mary, take a deep breath, and begin to relax a little as the curtain goes up.

Small skits are performed and there is the usual yelling, spitting, and noise. This theater doesn't seem to be any different than the Bowery Theater, except it might be more extravagant with the ornate gas lamps and cushioned seats. The seats feel like velvet and because the skits aren't that interesting to me, I drift into my own thoughts. I imagine myself climbing out of a grand and elegant carriage with my friends. I stroke my hands and pretend they're wearing the soft and pure white gloves the women wear at the Broadway Theater. And then after the Shakespeare play, I picture us climbing back into our carriage and going to a glittering ballroom in one of the fancy houses blazing with candlelight. I'll be wearing a gown made of pink taffeta . . .

"Nora! What are you doing with your hands? Why aren't you laughing? Aren't these the funniest actors . . . ," Mary says to me, interrupting my reverie. Sean presses close to me and I smell his breath. It smells like tobacco and I fear he's becoming an addict like the old Irish ladies I see in the streets selling apples and smoking pipes.

"It'd be grand if you could accompany Mary and me to the theater," Sean says. "You're not acting like you're with us now."

"I'm sitting right here and it still doesn't please you," I say, laughing. I'm not about to share with them what I've just dreamed up. They'd think I was being foolish and too high minded. I have nowhere to go but up and I'm not going to stop dreaming, even if Sean and Mary don't go with me.

The skits are finally over, the curtain comes down, and there's an intermission. Sean pulls out ham sandwiches and Mary has a flask of tea for us. I'm uncomfortable because I forgot to bring something to share. I guess I've become a bit stingy saving my money for Ireland.

Sean talks to some newsies he used to work with, but I don't know any of them. I look around and see working girls with bad reputations sitting amongst some fancy looking men. I've seen these girls on the streets and Mary has pointed them out to me as scandalous hookers. I also notice a few slick looking B'Hoys with their G'Hals on their arms. They make me cringe, for they think they're a higher class than someone like Mary and me, but they're worse than us. They're crude and putting on airs as if they're rich and important people of the city. Peanut shells are flying around and I only see two gloved women in the audience. I wonder how they've come to wear gloves and why they aren't at the Broadway Theater. The curtain goes up again and it's time for Shakespeare! To my disappointment, especially after having to endure the lowbrow acting in the skits, I see there is yet another skit!

"Look, it's Frank Chanfrau up there! He's from Five Points and he's the one helping us organize our own theater. I heard him and some others talking about his new act. This must be it!" Sean whispers loudly. For once the people in the theater are quiet for they sense there is something new they're about to see.

This Mr. Chanfrau strides onto the stage in a fireman's red jacket, wearing tight pants, and soap locked hair. Oh no, not someone playing a B'Hoy! A cigar is in his mouth and he takes it out in a haughty way and says, "I ain't a goin' to run with dat mercheen no more!" Everyone knows he is referring to his fire company. The crowd roars and claps in approval. Then he says, "I love that ingine better than my dinner." Again, the crowd roars. And then he says, "If I don't have a muss soon I'll spile!" He is speaking of being in a fight. The B'Hoys love their position in the city as firemen, for it's an esteemed job to have. But they also love fighting. How anyone would love fighting, I don't understand.

"His character is Mose and his gal is coming out now. Here she is! Look, Nora . . . Mary . . . look at her. Her character's name is Lize!" Sean exclaims.

Although the entire theater is vibrating with laughter and approval for this act, I'm only mildly amused. Is there to be no Shakespeare play? I wish we'd gone to the Bowery Theater instead of this new one. I should have known that having a gang member spit at me on my way to the theater was an omen that the evening was going to be spoiled. The curtain comes down and the boisterous theater goers are standing up applauding and shouting. Sean nods at us that we should leave before we get stampeded by the crowd. As we begin walking down the stairs, the noisy crowd grows quiet in the theater and there are whispers that the curtain has gone up again. There's more, they're saying.

"Look, there's an African on stage! There's someone else, too. There's going to be dancing!" people are shouting.

I leave Sean and Mary in the stairway and make my way back to the balcony. I'm not going to miss the dancing!

More people have come out on stage and then I see Da sitting there with his fiddle! Another surprise from Da! There is an African with a banjo and another one with a tambourine, the same man I saw at the dance hall playing with Da. My Da on stage in the Chatham Theater! He didn't bother to tell us that he was becoming someone famous playing his fiddle in a theater! I sit down in my seat, as does everyone else in the theater. I hardly notice that Mary and Sean have come to sit next to me. I feel excitement building up inside of me as I anticipate this new dance show. The African looks to be a young man, tall with skin as black as coal. He is wearing a vest, a long white coat, and shiny black boots with big heels on them. Standing next to him is another man who is as light-skinned as the African is dark. He is wearing a vest, black pants, a cravat, a top hat, and a fancy black jacket. Another man comes on stage who is dressed in fancy clothes and he motions with his hands for the people to sit down.

"Folks, you'll be getting your money's worth at the Chatham tonight, for we have a special grand finale for you. There's going to be a dance competition between two well known dancers standing here before you."

The emcee points to the African man and says, "Here is a man who can tie his legs into knots, all the while he dances to a jig, and of course, adding his own special inventions on the dance floor. May I present to you the phenomenal Master Juba!"

People in the crowd cheer and I think it's strange to have this well known African dancer approved of by mostly a white crowd. In the back of the theater, there's a small section reserved just for black people whose roots are from Africa. They are all standing, shouting, and clapping, but they have been given the worst seats in the theater.

"And may I present to you one of the great jig dancers the world has ever known, Mr. John Diamond!"

The crowd roars even louder and stomps and cheers. The emcee motions for people to sit down.

After it has quieted down, my Da and the other fiddler begin to play and Mr. Diamond dances, slowly at first, but then erupting into such frantic footwork, it's as if lightning has struck the floor, cracking the place open. He dances for a few minutes and then stops. Master Juba begins with a single shuffle, double shuffle, cutting and crossing, snapping his fingers, rolling his eyes, turning in his knees, and spinning. Da isn't fiddling for him, but the other fiddler and the tambourine man are making the music for his feet. And when he finishes after a few thrilling minutes, the musicians play together and both dancers begin striking the ground very rapidly with their heels and then toes, looking at one another and laughing, challenging each other with vigorous footwork. There is high stepping, foot stomping, and joyous fury in their steps alone and together. The crowd dances in the aisles, shouting, singing, clapping, and it is as if the world, another new world I've entered, has gone wild. I can't seem to get up from my seat, although Mary and Sean are up and dancing together in the aisle with everyone else, trying to imitate the dance masters on stage. I'm shocked to see Da on stage and mesmerized by the dance steps filled with grace and power that are electrifying the whole theater.

After the show, people dance and sing as they leave the theater. I don't try to go to my Da on stage because it's too crowded. As much as I will want to wait up for him tonight to ask him about his new job at the theater, I'll let him keep his secret. I have my secret, too, and we both possess these secrets for good reasons. Do I really believe this? I hope I do because I can feel my life careening into something new and a bit frightening.

The three of us don't say much as we walk home together. I figure that we're all touched by the magic of the evening and can't talk, but I'm displeased that Sean walked me home first. When I wave goodbye to my friends from the window of the apartment and watch them walk down the street, I think I see their hands come together. Or did I imagine it?

Chapter Nineteen

A Ticket for Nora

Breathes there the man with soul so dead
Who never to himself hath said:
"This is my own, my native land"?
Whose heart hath ne'er within him burned
As home his footsteps he hath turned
From wandering on a foreign strand?
—Sir Walter Scott

My memorable crystal winter in New York City is surrendering to spring's burgeoning warmth and growth. Tiny yellow dandelions peek through crevices in the broken and dirty sidewalks and violets grow in clumps wherever there might be a small patch of grass. I make bouquets to bring home to Mam, but when she returns from work they've wilted and drooped down, just like we all feel by the end of a day. Last spring, I didn't see beauty in my new world of New York, but this year it is as if God and his fairies are opening my eyes to see it all around me.

Meg is working in a little shop selling shoes and hats; some of the hats in her store are wearing the flowers I have made for them. She is wearing some fancy clothes these days and promised me she'd buy me a hat for my birthday, which will be before I leave for Ireland. I am still dreaming and scheming to go and have already bought my ticket through the Association. I lied about my age and told them I was sixteen; otherwise they wouldn't have sold me the ticket. My departure date is for May 14th. I have hid the ticket in my dresser and look at it every night before I go to sleep. A ticket to Ireland! I can't believe I have used up a lot of my savings to finally buy a ticket to go home. I feel strength in my decision, but I'm also terrified of leaving my family and going on a ship again. I was told by the Association that the ship I'll be traveling on is not a cattle ship this time, but a real passenger ship. I'll have my own private berth to sleep in. I thought about purchasing a return ticket, but I decided not to. I know Da and Mam will come back to Ireland once I'm there awhile. I honestly don't know how I will make money once I'm home in Ireland. I plan on bringing the rest of my savings with me to buy a few hens. Maybe I can be hired at one of the big houses doing piece work, especially since I now have experience working in America. I hate sewing, but I could pass for a seamstress if I wanted to. Before I fall to sleep at night, I imagine myself in Ireland sitting by the hearth in the evenings at our cottage doing some sewing on the fancy clothes from one of the big houses. The sun will be setting and I'll have my cup of tea next to me, waiting for Mam and Da to come home. I don't want to leave my dresser, but I know Da won't let anything happen to it and he'll bring it to Ireland when he and Mam come. I don't know if Meg will come back to Ireland, for she is feeling quite the success with her new work and having made a few friends here.

Da is always working or playing his fiddle, but I never did see his name on the marquee at the theater. I suppose it takes more than playing a fiddle in a theater to become famous. He never mentions going to California, but I heard him arguing with Mam one night about going. I think he's still planning on a short trip to dig for gold and then returning home as soon as he can.

I see my poor Mam's face lined with worry and concern. She is different now, and although she doesn't express her worry for all of us, I see it in her face. Her red hair is mostly white and she looks worn out and much older, but she's as lovely as any of the aristocratic ladies getting in and out of fancy carriages. Da occasionally brings her home special things like new utensils and exotic food. Sometimes he brings her home a bouquet of flowers from one of the vendors and she blushes like a young girl when he presents them to her. Then she scolds him, claiming she's worried about not being able to pay their rent or buy food because he's being frivolous when he buys her gifts. I know she loves it and is only pretending she doesn't.

Sean, Mary, and I went to the theater every couple of weeks all winter, but lately Sean has been too busy at the docks to go. Neither of them bought a ticket to go back to Ireland with me, although they know I have mine. They know the date I'm leaving and Sean said he thinks he knows the ship I'll be on. He and Mary are distant in their friendship towards me these days. Mary and I don't laugh and tell stories on the way home from school like we used to. She is working at the orphanage helping the younger children and said that if she didn't do this work, they'd be sending her off to find another place to live. She talks about getting married and thinks this will free her from the drudgery of working and living at the orphanage. She is seventeen and I suppose old enough to marry, but I tell her that her troubles will only increase, especially if she marries just to escape her surroundings.

Mrs. Drake is pleased with my work and has passed me to the next grade. I didn't have the heart to tell her that I'll be going to school in Ireland come September, and not in New York. She has a special fondness for me, and even if she's a do-gooder Protestant from a wealthy family, I like her. She's always encouraging me to try and get my stories and poems printed in one of the newspapers here in New York. I don't think the papers would want to publish a story written by Irish rabble, as they think we all are. I'd have to change my last name and I'm not willing to go that far, although many of the Irish, like Sean, have changed their names so they don't sound too Irish.

My legs have been growing and I'm not as short as I used to be. It must be the American food and air! Something else has been growing in New York, too. There is a growing hatred amongst theater goers in Five Points and the Bowery towards the newly built Astor Opera House. It's a grand opera house that stands south of Union Square. It stands at a point where the world of the Bowery and all of us struggling foreigners meander around, and Broadway, where the fashionable and wealthy parade about. It all began with two actors, but it really began way before these two men ever lived. It was seething in the bowels of Ireland and England for hundreds of years and now has chosen America to spill out its venom. These two actors just happen to be at the wrong place at the right time or the right place and the wrong time. I don't know. I don't pretend to be anyone I am not, and just because I am of Ireland, in America this means I am viewed as lowly scum. However, there is a difference. We are scum with hope because we are in America and America is a place for the impossible, for dreams to come true, and for the lowly to rise above the sewers of the Bowery. Maybe it's the muck we live in that is so fertile, like dirt, that it makes us dream and grow and not give up. I think hatred is like the blight that happens just before there's something wonderful ready to bloom. Sometimes we just can't wait any longer for the blooming, and because we're feeling the sunlight ready to bring it forth, we become impatient with the mire we're in. I can see it happening in this city. The Irish born and the Irish

Americans can't wait for growth. Perhaps they don't believe in growth that comes from good things like what is in the soil to make potatoes grow healthy. They feel all alone and must fight for growth and change.

These days, Five Points with its dark world of possibilities is feeling restless and angry. Since the splendid Astor Opera House was built between the two worlds—the world of the rich and the world of the poor—it has gotten worse. I guess you might say that the music, dancing, and entertainment are so popular in our impoverished part of this city, it too is ready to burst fully into the sunlight. There are people from all around the city that flock to our world to experience this jubilant night life, even with the stench of evil that clings to it. I become confused by it all. I look at the Astor Opera House and long to put on an evening dress and kid gloves to go there to see a play. And then I chastise myself for feeling this way, for it is the other theaters, the working class theaters that I'm most comfortable in. I've made memories in these theaters and my Da sometimes plays fiddle for the dance competitions. I often think that after I return to Ireland, I'll work and save my money to open up a theater in Cork. I've had a taste now for the grand life here in America and I aim to take it home with me to Ireland.

On this fine evening in May, my friends and I are sitting at a performance at the Broadway Theater. Tonight will be my last trip to the theater in New York and I won't be seeing my friends for a long time, perhaps never again. When there is possibility for loss of family and friends, it hurts deeper than ever. Although I'm angry at them for not going with me, my sadness is greater than my anger. I leave for Ireland in a few days. I found a used carpet bag to stuff all my belongings into and I'm ready to go! I haven't been able to eat very much in the last week; my nerves are fraying and unraveling in my belly. It is there I feel everything, as if my heart and belly become one with the intensity of my feelings. I wonder if I will have the courage to leave my family! These thoughts fly around my head and prevent me from enjoying being out with my friends. The tickets were expensive, but well worth it for we are being treated to our own Five Points actor, Edwin Forrest. He is famous for playing firemen and patriotic heroes who rescue helpless women. He also performs the high brow plays, such as Shakespeare, and tonight we are watching a performance of Macbeth. There's a riotous and restless spirit filling the theater this night. Mr. Forrest and the famous English actor William Charles Macready have been in a war with words with each other for a year or so. Macready has criticized Forrest and says he lacks taste and is vulgar in his acting. Forrest said that Macready is an aristocratic codfish. When Macready is playing in the States, Forrest and his friends hiss and boo at him during his performance. Macready also tries to interrupt Forrest when he plays in England. It doesn't help that they play in competing productions, such as Macbeth.

There is an old warrior spirit seething in the Irish who have been forced to travel here because of British hatred. We have been finding our own voice and don't relish having the British telling us we are vulgar and lack gentility to perform proper Shakespeare. Da despises the Irish who resort to violence to fight British hatred, but I am beginning to understand why they do it. Will the British follow us to America to destroy us here, too? Mary believes that we Irish are too sensitive and given to exaggerating the facts, but our new world in America is giving us hopeful sunlight and we aren't about to let the British take this away from us. We aren't about to have this growth forbidden to break through to the sun and be forced back down in the mire. We are ready and I can feel it. We all can feel it. All of us— the Irish born and the Irish born in America. We are becoming united in this spirit although we don't really understand it fully. I wish my Da had time to talk to me about these things. I have thought about talking to Mrs. Drake, but she is too busy with her students. Maybe I'll run into Mr. Whitman again and see what he thinks about Macready and Forrest.

"Do you always have to sit between Sean and me, Nora?" Mary whispers in my ear.

"Do you fancy him?" I come right out and ask Mary.

"I do not!"

"You always want to sit next to him."

"I don't. I'm curious as to why you must always sit next to him. Do you fancy him?" Mary asks in a very loud whisper.

"Who fancies who?" Sean leans over us both with a big grin on his face.

"Ladies and Gentlemen . . . you are about to see a spectacular version of Macbeth performed by one of our very own superb and talented actors, Edwin Forrest!" the emcee announces.

"Saved by the emcee!" Mary whispers to me. I laugh and think how silly we are being. Of course we're only friends and we do fancy one another, but not in a romantic sense. I settle myself into my seat for the show. I haven't seen Macbeth before, but Mrs. Drake has been reading some of it in class.

"Our Mr. Forrest is not genteel, subdued, or refined as our Mr. Macready has accused him of NOT being, but indeed is vulgar and the best darn actor this side of the sea and the other side of the sea as well!" the emcee shouts.

Cheers and applause explode in the theater. Sean and Mary stand to their feet, but I don't get up. The emcee is just going to make matters worse between Macready and Forrest.

"Stand up, Nora!" Sean shouts down at me. "Stand up!"

I stand up and say to Sean, "Taking sides is wrong, and it'll only make everyone get more worked up."

"For once we're not alone in disliking the British. We have the power here, Nora. Can't you see it? All of us, whether born here or over there won't put up with their kind telling us we're worthless and no good at our theater acting. The Astor place shouldn't have been built. It's keeping us out, making us having to wear fancy clothes and telling us we're not wanted because we're Irish scum. It won't be like Ireland again, Nora. America won't allow it. And you know why? Because we Irish have started our own country here, Nora. There are more Irish here in New York than in Ireland! We won't be having the British keeping us from the big houses here in New York!"

Sean lifts his hands in the air, makes fists, and cheers and hollers like everyone else. He stomps and goes into the aisle with Mary alongside of him. I feel nothing. I agree that coming all the way here to escape British hatred and then to experience it here is wrong. And yet I can't participate in this angry cheering. I must have my Da's self-control and stubbornness. There were many times in Ireland Da wanted to take up arms against the British, but he chose not to. He said that those who take up the sword will die by the sword, and more times than not, it was what we saw in Ireland.

The theater eventually quiets down and we sit enjoying every line of Macbeth. How I love Mr. Shakespeare's words! He tells the stories of the mighty and the lowly, bringing them equality through humor and blazing truth. It's as if we see ourselves raised high above the characters as we watch them act out silliness and stupidity. We see that the kings and queens, as well as the court jesters and servants, are all subject to the same passions and problems. We laugh at ourselves as we watch a Shakespeare play.

Mr. Shakespeare can certainly honey up the sins of people with such elegant words. For a time, I forget the ache in my heart because I'm leaving New York, my family, and friends.

And then Mr. Forrest bellows out, "What rhubarb, senna, or what purgative drug will scour these English hence?" and the entire audience roars and cheers, standing to their feet again, but this time with curses spewing forth from their mouths against the English. Sean and Mary are up, too, and participating in the uproar. I am dumbfounded and don't know what to think. Mr. Forrest says the line again before going on. Eventually everyone quiets down and listens to the rest of the play.

After we leave the theater, there are crowds of people walking towards the Astor Opera House. They're chanting, "Down with codfish aristocracy!" repeatedly. All around me are people with rocks, brick bats, well dressed and ragged, but mostly there are poor and tired looking people, hard working class people who are red in the face and bellowing out obscenities. The people of New York seem to have gone mad and most of these people appear to be Irish.

"There's a riot at the Astor! Himself (speaking of Macready, Forrest's rival) left out the back door!" someone shouts out to those gawking in confusion at the crowd.

"I want to go home. I want to go home now!" I yell at Sean and Mary, and run down the street. I stumble and fall right into some boys carrying bats.

"Where ya goin', miss? Ya goin' to a fire at the Astor?" one of them says to me, laughing. The others laugh at me, too, while I'm sprawled out on the road.

Sean comes to my side and helps me up. Tears flow freely down my cheeks. I'll be glad to leave this wicked country, I think.

"If there's a fire, it'll burn the city. New York catches fire easily!" I cry.

"There'll be no fire," Sean says as he holds me close to his side. "We have enough firemen here in this city to fill the whole state of New York."

We make our way through the crowds towards my home. Carriages fly by and policemen fill the streets and tell everyone to go home. Mary comes up alongside me and takes my arm. I suddenly feel loved and protected by my friends while all around me there is chaos and anger filling the streets. It's as if this city requires winter snow to bury its differences and sorrows, and now that spring is here, the air is humid and filled with warlike cries and anger. It should be filled with hope now that flowers are springing up from the earth. We say goodbye to Mary at the corner of Chatham Square and Dover Street. She has met someone from the orphanage who is going to walk with her the rest of the way home.

There's a group of men assembled in front of Jim McNulty's Saloon and Sean directs me right inside. We find a small table to sit at amongst the agitated crowd filling the small business. I shouldn't be in a saloon, especially where there's no room for the dancing and fiddling. There's something dark and energetic in the room and all I want to do is go home. I begin shaking, but Sean doesn't notice because he's fascinated watching the people in the room who are mostly men.

"Rynders meets with the men of the Bowery and Five Points here," Sean says. "He might be coming tonight. He has a mighty sway over people." He slams his hand down on the table and then onto his knee. "You might see history made tonight, Nora!"

"I don't trust Mr. Rynders," I reply.

A saloon keeper comes to our table and says to Sean, "Ya can't be sittin here warmin' your bums without purchasing a pint."

"A pint for me and a hot chocolate for the lady," Sean says proudly.

"Righto," he replies.

"What's wrong with you?" I ask Sean. "Are you mad? This place is swarming with angry men all talking about the Astor place. There's going to be a riot. I know it. There's going to be a riot and a fire and none of us will survive."

"This city is eternal. It'll survive," Sean says as he looks all around him.

"But will we?"

"We're Irish . . . we'll survive."

"So now you're acknowledging you're Irish, Sean O," I say, laughing just a little.

The bartender brings us our drinks and Sean pays him, giving him a large tip.

"You need to be saving, not spending," I lecture him.

"There's plenty more from where it came from. I'm not a bit worried."

"What about Ireland? You promised . . ."

"It's a foolish time to go back to the ole country," he interrupts. "There's still a Famine going on, which is one of the reasons why we don't want to see no English actor lord it over us with kid gloves at the Astor place."

"My cousin writes that our cottage is still standing and things are better in Cork."

"It's still not over. As long as the English are in control, it won't be over."

"Then we should be helping Ireland get control."

"You're daft, Nora! How many hundreds of years have the Irish fought the English?"

"America fought them and won."

"They didn't fight for hundreds of years. And Ireland is no America, is it now?"

"I'm going. I've my ticket and I board in a few days," I say, my heart aching something fierce as I think of leaving.

"I can't stop you, but what about your family? I can't be keeping it from them. They might come asking me. You have to tell them, or they'll be killed from worrying."

"I'm leaving a note in the dresser and I'm hoping you'll go to them the next day. Convince them that I'm on a safe ship and I'll be grand."

"I will. I'll do it for you, Nora. Do ya have a return ticket, now?"

"No," I say, tears splashing out of my eyes.

Sean reaches for my hands across the table. "I won't be sleeping again until you're back here, wee one."

"So you'll not be sleeping, then." I pull away from him and place my hands over my face to have a good cry. I'm not even embarrassed to be crying in front of Sean in a public place.

Sean pulls my hands away and leans closer to me from across the table. "What is it that possesses a girl to want to go back to the blackened potatoes and destitution of her country?"

"Do you remember the story about the swallow that returns from Africa to Ireland every year to the same place it was born? Every year, as long as it lives, it returns to its home. How can any journey be too long when you're going home? Do you remember any of your Irish language? In Irish it's said, *'Nil aon tinnean mar do thinntean fein.'* 'There is no hearth like the hearth at home.'"

Chapter Twenty

Chaos in New York City

Comfort every sufferer
Watching late in pain;
Those who plan some evil,
From their sin restrain.
—Sabine Baring-Gould

Sean walks me home and to the door of our apartment. He is giving me a kiss on the cheek when Meg opens the door.

"And what do we have here? A little smooching for a girl barely out of her nappies!"

"Mam!" Meg yells back into the apartment, "It's our Nora giving a kiss to a lad!" Then she shuts the door on us.

"Never mind her," I say to Sean. "She's jealous because she's an old maid! I'll just let her think you're my boyfriend."

"I'm not? I thought I was your special lad," Sean says.

I'm surprised by Sean's words! I don't ever want to marry anyone, but if I did, I would first have to have someone special. I wonder if Sean is asking to be my special lad. Will this make my heart strong to go back to Ireland knowing he's here waiting and caring for me? Will it shake my confidence in leaving without a return ticket? These feelings flood me in a moment's time while Sean stands before me.

The door opens again and Mam is before us looking angry and worried.

"Come in now, Nora. It's too late for you to be out. I was worried for you. 'Tis bad enough I must worry about your Da being out late playing his music. I'll not have my youngest running the streets!"

"I've not been running the streets. We went to the theater—Mary, Sean, and I went to see a play and we've just come home. I told you where we were going. Sean only gave me a kiss on the cheek. Don't believe Meg and her lies!" I whisper loudly because the other tenants are probably listening at their doors.

"Go home now, Sean. You'll be waking the neighbors with this carrying on," Mam says as she motions for me to come in while dismissing Sean.

"I'm sorry to disturb you, Mrs. McCabe. I'll be going now. Bye, Nora." Sean takes his cap off and when he nods goodbye, I think I see tears in his eyes.

I sit by my dresser, light the candle, and write my family a long letter about why I'm going back to Ireland. Tears smear the paper I'm writing on, rough brown paper the butcher had wrapped our meat in. The stub of a charcoal pencil Mrs. Drake gave me to write my stories with is uncomfortable in my hand. Mam and Meg haven't gone to sleep yet and are mumbling something to each other in the dark.

"Don't be using up the candle, Nora. Save the light for when we need it most," Meg says loudly.

"Let her be," Mam responds. "Nora needs to curse her darkness by writing out her feelings. We'll be buying more candles."

"When is Da coming home, Mam?" I ask. I want to tell her about seeing him on stage playing at the theater, but I don't.

"The saloons are open all night. He's making a pretty penny playing his fiddle in them. Blow out the candle soon and go to sleep, and don't be minding about your Da."

"God bless you, Mam."

I finish the letter, trying not to make noise as I cry. I go to sleep listening to the sounds in the streets that are louder than usual tonight. I think sweetly and sadly that soon I shall hear the magpie and the song of the lark when I fall asleep in our cottage in Ireland. The fields will be green and full of wildflowers to pick for my hair. I will find my old friends and lay down in the dew to make myself beautiful. But it is my heart that is bothering me, breaking from love for my family, even my Meg. There might be a crack or two there that is broken for Sean as well, and of course, for my friend, Mary. I wonder if there is one for this city I'll be leaving. Will I miss this city that is sometimes filled with sparkling promise from the stars that shine down upon it?

Within the next few days, I learn that I've been right about the spirit of this city changing from lively revelry to dark foreboding. There must have been demons flying about when Macbeth was performed in both the Chatham and Astor theaters that night. Maybe the witches from the play left the stage to agitate the minds of the susceptible. But were these witches from the Chatham or the Astor? And are they Protestant or Catholic, English, American, or Irish? Since that night, the city streets haven't been safe and the newspapers have headlines such as, "Shall Americans or English Rule in this City?" Everyone in Five Points is calling the Astor Opera House, "The English Aristocratic Opera House." There's going to be a riot. Anyone can see it coming, but no one seems to want to stop it. There are only two voices, two sides, and two powers, in all of this. There is the mayor and prominent people in the city, including some writers as the popular Washington Irving, who are saying that Macready, the English actor, should return to the Astor Theater to do Macbeth again! They say that he shouldn't be intimidated by the dirty rabble-rousers. And then there is Captain Isaiah Rynders, who owns the Empire Club and is always whipping up support for the Democratic party, trying to win over Five Points. He's a bully, and when there's an election, he has his men beat up people who don't vote the way he wants them to. This Rynders uses intimidation and outright violence to get votes. Even though Da says the Democratic Party is the right way to go for us Irish, he says it's wrong for this Rynders to come into our part of the city and force us to vote a certain way. Da doesn't like the mayor or Rynders and he wants Macready run out of town, too. As I walk to school and home again, I've been frightened by all the handbills posted saying that if Macready performs Macbeth again, there'll be trouble.

I've just said goodbye to Mary who promised to meet me on the morning I leave for Ireland three days from today! It will be one of the hardest things I've ever done in my life, so I'm pleased Sean and Mary will be seeing me off. I look up into the sky and there are no clouds at all. The tall buildings look like claws reaching towards heaven as they glimmer in the sunlight. I feel like skipping. The air is warm and I smell the earth longing to push flowers and grass right through the city streets between the throngs of people being too busy to notice sunlight splashing on the earth to make it happy. I'm hopeful that maybe Macready will perform and then go home to England and there won't be any trouble after all. How could there be such trouble on a spring day as lovely as this one?

A newsboy is hawking papers and I decide to buy one to bring home to Da. I buy the *Herald* and an apple from a vendor and lean up against one of the buildings to take a look at the paper. I turn to the talk of the town section, called "Prittle Prattle" that is supposed to be New York's exclusive column. This column is intended to keep the city's refined individuals apprised of all that is new, charming and instructive on the brilliant circle of city life. I laugh to myself when I read this, figuring it isn't meant for the likes of someone like me. It describes the play "Erami" that opened in November at the Astor amid blazing jewels and rustling silk for New York's "haut monde." I don't know what "haut monde" means, but it must mean it's only for the rich and high and mighty of the city, keeping the Irish rabble out. And then it says that Macready will be performing tonight, May 10th, for the city's refined and genteel theater goers. I throw the paper down and stomp on it. I wish I hadn't wasted my money buying the darn thing! I don't want Da reading about the uppertons and feeling low! Just the way they write about the play is a slap in our faces, intimidating us, and suggesting we stay away from the rich and elite of the city. No wonder there's uproar against this actor! I've a mind to get myself a brick bat and go there tonight!

I walk towards home and remember this is the night that my Da plays in the Broadway Theater during the intermissions. I'm glad he won't be anywhere near the Astor, but maybe Sean won't be able to keep himself away. I have a mind to go to the Astor myself, but I have to ready myself for the long journey on the ship. I shouldn't get worked up about these things happening here, for I'll soon be gone. I look up into the sky and decide not to think about Macready and a riot any longer. I need my wits about me to get on that ship for Ireland! Ireland! My anticipation and excitement is growing and getting stronger, and it is beginning to put my sadness about leaving in its proper place. I am going home!

Later that night after Mam and Meg have gone out visiting, I sit next to my dresser. I stick my head inside and hear the ocean breathing from within the walls. I smell the salty sea and hear Maggie whispering to me that I can come out of the dresser to go on deck to get some fresh air. I am sad that I no longer can fit my whole body inside. Mam's old shawl has never left the dresser since she gave it to me before leaving Ireland. I pull it out of the corner of the dresser and lay my head down on it. I close my eyes but don't feel cradled and protected. Is it because I can't fit my whole body inside, or is it because I will not be able to have the dresser with me when I'm on the ship? My head begins to spin with worry and fear. Then there is louder than usual noise outside the window. I squeeze my eyes shut and pray, and soon I am sleeping and forgetting all my troubles.

A couple of hours later I wake up to someone banging on the door. I recognize Sean's voice shouting for someone to open up the door. I pull my head out of the dresser and try to get up, feeling terribly stiff.

I open the door and Sean stands there with his hair sticking up all over his head. I almost laugh because he looks like a frightened porcupine, a red one at that.

"What in the name of God are you doing here?" I ask.

"Can I come in? Is anyone here?" he asks nervously, craning his head to look inside.

"No one's here. You can come in," I say, as I open the door for him to come inside. I think of Da warning me not to open the door to just anyone. Is Sean just anyone? No, he isn't, I think warmly.

Sean comes in and walks over to the dresser. I can't remember if he has seen it before or not. He stares at it, touches it, and then turns to me.

"I've not seen a dresser since I left Ireland. I didn't know you had one here."

"'Tis my own dresser, Sean. It kept me safe on the ship coming over."

Sean walks to the table and sits down, putting his head in his hands.

"What's wrong?" I ask.

He lifts his head and stares at me while I wait for him to say something.

"It's Da. I mean, it's your Da, Nora."

I rush over to the table and yell, "What about Da?"

"He's somewhere in the mess out there," Sean says as he stands up. "There's a riot at the Astor and he was one of the musicians playing during intermission."

"Da doesn't play at the Astor. He plays at the Broadway." I begin shaking all over.

"He got a wad of money to play there tonight because none of the other musicians would do it. They knew there'd be trouble, but your Da was the only one who'd play."

"How do you know? You aren't on speaking terms with my Da. How would you know where he was playing? He told me he was playing at the Broadway. I'm going to go find him there!" I begin putting my boots on and Sean pulls on my arm.

"You aren't going out there. Hell has broken loose on the streets. Where are your Mam and sister?"

I try to calm myself to answer him. "Mam and Meg are at the O'Gradys' down the street."

"I want you to stay here while I go tell them they need to come home and stay inside until this blows over."

"Tell me more about Da," I say, tears rolling down my cheeks as I shake all over.

"I ran into him tonight on Chatham Street. He told me about playing at the Astor for a lot of money."

"Maybe he'll be showing up here any minute then. He must have gotten out a back door. He'll be here soon. I know it. Everything's going to be okay. Everyone around here knows my Da isn't a troublemaker and no one will hurt him." Hope flares up momentarily.

I look at Sean and know he's keeping something else from me.

"Tell me! Tell me what you know, Sean O'Connolly!"

"Rynders and his men made threats that if any Irish musician played for Macready, he'd be sorry." Sean walks back and forth in front of me, looking down.

"I'll look for him. Your Da. I'll look for him. Stay here and don't leave the building!" Sean quickly kisses me on the cheek and leaves.

I sit and pound my fists so hard on the table that Paws, who has been lying in the corner sleeping, jumps up and runs inside the dresser. Nothing can happen to my Da now! He's happy playing his fiddle and trying to make money for us. Nothing can happen to my Da! I get up from the table and wrap the blue scarf around my neck before I hurry out the door and down the steps to make my way to the Astor. The air is dense with smoke and I hear screaming and shouting in the distance. I start to run, but hesitate and walk back to our apartment. When I go inside, I peer into the dresser and see Paws, his sad green eyes lighting up the dark when he looks up at me.

"'Tis only a minor setback, Paws. It'll be grand soon," I say to him. I find the coin Da gave me long ago before I climbed into the dresser to board the *Star* to go to America and put it in my pocket for good luck.

Chapter Twenty-one

AN ANCIENT WARRIOR

Cúchulainn stirred,
Stared on the horses of the sea, and heard
The cars of battle and his own name cried;
And fought with the invulnerable tide
—W. B. Yeats, "Cúchulainn's Fight with the Sea"

As I rush through the streets, I bump into people meandering around in a daze. Some of them are holding torches over their heads, yelling and commanding the people following them. Many of the gas lamps have been destroyed and shards of glass glitter in the moonlight. I stop in the middle of a street and look up into the sky just for a moment. I need to remember the world is bigger than this city. I'm surprised to see a full moon shining down upon the chaos of my city. My city? No, this moon is smiling at me, not at this crazy and mean city that is not my real home. The moon is giving me courage to find my Da. I begin following a group of men and women being led by someone who looks like he is walking on stilts. He towers above everyone else. His hair is reddish-brown and curling around his black leather cap that is too small for his head. He turns once to look back at the crowd following him and I am reminded of the great warrior, Cúchulainn. The traveling schoolmaster in Ireland would tell us stories about him around the hearth late

150

at night. I blindly follow this ancient warrior in the dark behind the crowd going towards the Astor Opera House. There is a stench of smoke mingling with sour sweat, cheap perfume, and rotting garbage that fills my nostrils. I cough and gag, and weep loudly and uncontrollably, not caring if anyone hears or sees me. These sounds mingle with the angry words of protest all around me. As we reach the Astor, it looks like thousands of people have gathered in front of the theater holding torches, shouting obscenities, and throwing rocks. They lift their arms over their heads and chant, "Burn the Astor! Burn the Astor!" I'm pushed and shoved by the crowd and can't see ahead of me. When I can finally look up over the heads before me, I see arms raised high, some with torches, some making fists, and it reminds me of great desperate prayers to God. Prayers of desperation from people who have no other way to make it understood that they will no longer endure being cast out of heaven on earth in their new country. These people are telling God they will fight for themselves even if He won't fight for them. They are taking matters into their own hands.

Someone knocks me to the ground and for a moment, I stay there unable to move. I think I might be trampled on if I don't try to get up, but I stay there on my knees and bow my head to pray. I pray to God and his fairies that I will live through this to find my Da who will live through this, too. I pray for help, clear and simple. "Help, please God!" I hear myself roar as if a lion was living deep inside of me. Suddenly an arm is reaching down for me and pulling me up. I cling to this strong arm as it pulls me up, up, above the crowd and onto the shoulders of what I think must be a giant. I soar above the crowd! And when I look down, I see that I am riding upon the warrior himself. It is the warrior, Cúchulainn, who has come for me. Anything can happen in America, I think! He strides through the crowd with me on his shoulders. I don't know where we are going, but I am transcended above the chaos and fighting all around us. I no longer feel frightened until gunfire explodes near us and there are flashes of light and nothing else. I hear my warrior tell me to hang on tight and that I'll be all right, but I must have been struck by some of the gun powder and now I'm blind! I hear screaming and someone shouting that people have been shot and killed. And when I hear someone shout that it looks like the musician from the Broadway Theater has been shot, I faint on the shoulders of my great warrior.

I awake on the floor next to my dresser to the sounds of weeping and praying. For a moment, I think I must be back in Ireland at a wake. I'm light-headed and disoriented, but I slowly sit up and look around the apartment. Mam, Meg, and some neighborhood women are sitting around the table with cups of tea, their heads in their hands, praying and crying. I know it has to be Da. Something terrible has happened to my Da!

"Where's Da?" I ask when I stand to my feet. The women stop praying and turn towards me. Mam comes to me and I see in her eyes that Da must be gone. She embraces me and holds me so tightly, I can't breathe. Her chin sticks into my shoulder blade and quivers with sobs. My Mam is a strong woman and her grip on me tells me she will still be strong through this. As the truth of Da being gone fills me with sorrow, I wonder how I'll go on. I've always felt that his spirit is a part of my own. His love of Ireland and his gentle and strong ways have influenced me in everything I do. I would not have picked up a rock to throw at the Astor Opera House or at the police beating back the people. I would not harm anyone, except someone harming my Da or my family and friends. But right now I feel rage for whoever killed my Da. The more I become aware that my Da is gone as Mam holds me, the more I feel a power within me to want to hurt and destroy whoever did this.

Mam lets me go and says, "Your Da ran out of the Astor when people were throwing furniture on stage. He ran out the back and when he was trying to come home, he got caught in the crowd." Mam sobs and puts her head in her hands. My mind can't fully register this news. I just stand there feeling as if I will faint again. Mam stops weeping and looks at me. "Then there were gun shots. People were killed, and one of them was your Da."

I fall down on my knees and notice that my dress is dirty and torn up the middle. I remember that I was sitting on a giant's shoulders and it must have ripped at that time.

"How do you know Da was one of them shot?" I ask.

One of the neighbor women, Mary, an old woman from Cork, gets up from the table and comes to stand by Mam.

"It was your guardian angel who told us, Nora. You might have been stampeded to death if he hadn't pulled you off the ground and onto his shoulders, thanks be to God for your man's kindness! It was him, the Lord bless and keep him, who brought you home and told us the fiddler named Eoin McCabe had been shot and killed, along with some others in the crowd."

Mary helps Mam back to the table to be consoled by the neighbor women. I bend over in prayer and can say nothing to God. My tears stop flowing and I realize that my ticket to Ireland is dear to me more than ever. I'll go back to Ireland for Da, for all of us. I stand up and walk over to the table where the women are weeping and praying.

"Where's his body?" I ask. They all look up and are silent.

"I want to see Da's body before I believe he's gone from us," I say with resolution.

Mam stands up and screams at me, "He's already buried! And without a proper wake!" She runs out into the hallway and Mary goes after her.

Meg gets up from the table and comes to me. Her eyes are swollen and as red as her hair. She grabs my arm and pulls me over near the dresser.

"This is Da's wake, Nora. Here . . . today, now even. People around Five Points are coming here today and into the evening to bring food and show their proper respects. The priest himself should be coming, too. Stop asking Mam questions. You have to be strong for her. We have to be strong, again, just like when we left Ireland and when we lost Kate."

"I want to talk to someone about this. How can you believe he's dead and been buried so soon? I have to go . . . ," I say as I begin to leave.

"No! You can't go and make our Mam sick with worry because you're out on the streets again," Meg yells while pulling my arm. "There's a curfew now . . . no one but the militia are allowed on the streets. There are fires around the city and people are angry. They're drunk and violent! You can't leave this apartment! Don't you even be thinking of running away!" Meg clasps me to her bosom and hugs me tightly.

Then she pushes me away and tells me to go for some water to wash myself. I turn to walk out the door to get some clean water. Mam has already come in and sat down again to her tea that she isn't drinking. She isn't crying, but looking stern and staring out the window. Before I walk out into the hallway, I hear her say, "It's time to go home. I'll be going home to Dublin soon."

Chapter Twenty-two

TIME TO WEEP NO MORE

My heart is in woe,
And my soul deep in trouble,—
For the mighty are low,
And abased are the noble:
the Sons of the Gael
Are in exile and mourning,
Worn, weary, and pale . . .
—Fearflatha O Gnimh,
"The Downfall of the Gael"

It's been two days since we had Da's wake in our apartment. I don't know how it could have been a proper wake without Da's body before us. We believe that when we hold our wakes, the spirit of the deceased is coaxed, prayed, and blessed out of the body and into heaven. There's nothing stingy in our weeping as we empty our sorrows without holding back. While my tears were being squeezed and wrung out of my soul all that day and night, I imagined my Da standing before me. I remembered being in Famine Ireland again when he came home from toiling on the road works. He was tired and thin, but his smile for me was all my own. I remembered looking at him and seeing the love of life he hadn't lost. I always heard it in his voice, in his fiddling, and in his gentleness towards me. I don't believe any other Irish child had a Da like my own. As I remembered him this way, my tears fell onto my freckled arms and I heard him say that I must have hope. Hope never ends and goes on forever. Hope dances in the darkness. And then I made a fool of myself and tried climbing into the dresser with half of me hanging out, but my head and heart were cradled inside of it. It is there I can find hope and believe in God and his fairies.

Sean came to the wake and told me about the mob of eight thousand poor people who had wanted to tear down the Astor Place Opera House. The militia was called in and a cannon was fired into the crowd. After it was all over, twenty-two people had died and more than one hundred and fifty were injured. Sean asked if I was still going to go to Ireland, and when I told him I was planning on boarding the ship, he said it would kill my mother to have me gone after my Da's death. I hadn't been thinking straight about this, for the loss of Da is greater than the sadness I feel for Mam and her loss. I heard her say she was going to go home to Dublin, but I didn't hear her say that Meg and I would be going with her. The neighbors say that Meg and I would be better off here in America. Mam agreed, but she said she needed to return to her home once more since Da died and then she'd come back here. Home is where we all long to go, but when we are finally home, there is something that makes us want to leave it, too. Home is where Mam wants to go, Da is in his home in heaven, Meg would like a home of her own here in America, and I still want to go home to Ireland. Now I want to go home especially for Da and not just for myself. I can't wait to see if Mam decides to go or not. I've written her a note and told her I'd be safe so she need not suffer any more loss. I know she'll understand, as she knows I'm no longer a child. And Mam knows that if I die, I'll be with Da and Kate in our real home in heaven.

Today is the day I set sail for Ireland. I move about in the early morning preparing to go, putting one foot in front of the other as a soldier would do. I feel numb and empty, but very determined. I told Sean and Mary that my heart would break in more parts than it already has if they came to see me off now. I said my goodbyes to them at the wake. It was a wake for more than my Da. It was a wake to say goodbye to America and my new life here. Once more, I squeeze part of myself into my dresser and find Da's coin to tuck into my pocket. I imagine I smell the salty sea again, hear Kate's laughter, Da's fiddling, Meg yelling at me to get out and help her, and Mam's stern voice telling me I am too big to be crawling in a dresser. In my note to Mam, I told her she must bring the dresser and Paws with her when she comes to Ireland. I will have my dresser in my heart now, for my hiding place has to be within me. It has to be one that no one can destroy or one I can't grow too big for. I kiss the bottom floor of the dresser, pet Paws who has been my faithful friend in America, and climb out. Mam is sitting at the window staring and Meg has gone to work. I walk up to Mam and touch her shoulder to get her to look at me. She is in a faraway and sad place, but I need her to really look at me and listen to me before I leave.

"I have to go, Mam. The curfew has lifted and New York is going to keep moving on, even if it might be a little ragged and worn out. It's a strong city and so am I. Don't worry for me." I give her a kiss and hug her. She hugs me back and smiles. As I leave the apartment and walk down the steps, Da's coin falls out of my pocket. I had been mindlessly touching it with one hand and carrying my bag in the other, and now I've carelessly dropped it. I get down on my knees on the steps to try and find it. I can't go to Ireland without Da's coin! I can't leave it here! It's my special magic coin of hope Da placed in my hand in Ireland when we were nearly starving to death. I can't take my dresser or Paws with me, but I must take Da's coin on the ship with me! I walk down the steps and try to reach behind them to where my coin must have dropped, but there is no opening. I climb back onto the steps and reach through the slats, my arms getting scratched from splinters. I go to each step and reach and reach, but my fingers don't find the coin.

By the time I have climbed to the top of the steps, I am sobbing and screaming. "God! Bring my Da back to me! I don't want to go home without him! I don't want to go without Da!" I roll down the steps and land on my belly on the sidewalk, not feeling any pain from the fall. I stay there crying and don't even care that there are children and people coming to watch my carrying on. I don't look up, but I feel them there and can hear them whispering about me. Then I think such a terrible thought that I can hardly breathe. I think that perhaps there is no such place as home, either here or in Ireland. Home is somewhere I can't really go to. Home is somewhere in the lines of a poem, sliding on the bow strings of Da's fiddle, in the snowflakes that tumble from a very narrow sky in New York City, and somewhere inside of me that is still being built with all the materials I have known in my life. There is such loud hammering in my brain as I think these things that I don't realize someone is pulling me up into their arms.

It is not the ancient Irish warrior, Cúchulainn, this time. These are arms that are thin, but very strong, sure, and gentle. These are familiar arms. These are my Da's arms, for he has not perished in the Astor Opera House riot and this is not a dream or a vision I'm having.

"Never have I loved you as I love you now, *a storin*," he says, clasping me to himself, barely able to hold me up as he used to, for I have grown out of being the wee one. I look over his shoulder and see all the people who have gathered on the street to watch this miracle of rebirth—my Da returning to us alive!

"Da's alive! He's alive!" I cry out to the people watching us.

Mam comes out of the apartment and stands at the top of the steps with her hand over her mouth to quell the sobs of joy and relief. Then she takes her hand away and cries out, "You've come home to us, Eion McCabe!" I've never seen my mother conduct herself in any way other than being proper, but she suddenly lifts her arms and jumps down from the top of the steps and lands in front of Da and me. Da reaches for her and the three of us hold on to each other for dear life. Our neighbors and friends are clapping and cheering, and someone tells us he'll go for Meg at the shop where she is working.

Chapter Twenty-three

CONCLUSION

It was as if Da had been brought back to life from a real death. Everyone thought he had been shot and killed by the militia, but it had been another fiddler killed in the riot. Da had been injured and in hospital with a concussion from falling onto a stone wall when the militia fired a cannon near him. No one had bothered telling us he was still alive, for the authorities don't really care about the life of an Irish man or woman. I have decided to give my ticket to go to Ireland to my warrior, Cúchulainn. He is coming for the grand celebration today in Five Points in honor of my Da rising from the ashes of the Astor Opera House Riot. His real name is Frank O'Dooley, and he came from Ireland a few years ago. No one messes with Frank O'Dooley in New York, but he wants to go back to Ireland something fierce. I still want to return home to Ireland, but not as fiercely as Frank does. Not anymore. For now, my home is here in New York with my Da, Mam, and Meg. Da has promised us that he won't go to California to dig for gold. "All my gold is right here," he said.

There is whispering that some uppertons, those codfish aristocracy, have come slumming into Five Points. They've come to the *céilí* we're having on the street before our apartment. The mayor of New York has given us permission to close down the street to traffic for a few hours so we can show New York how to really celebrate life with music and making our feet sing.

I look around me on this warm spring evening and can imagine the fairies weaving their magic between us all. There are Germans, Italians, Africans, and yes, I do believe I see Lavonia and her friends who had taken me to the Barnum Museum, climb out of their Cinderella carriage to come join us. As I swing Sean in waltz hold, I look up into the sky at the glimmering stars pulsating in rhythm to the music, and I know that either here or in Ireland, God and his fairies will always be where I am.

Educational Resources

LESSON PLANS: IMMIGRATION
Learn, Accept, Celebrate, Overcome

Goal: *Learn* about immigration—past and present; *Accept* diversity; *Celebrate* contributions; *Overcome* prejudice

Objectives: *Students will:* **Read** *Hope in New York City: The Continuing Story of The Irish Dresser* and other fiction about immigration (see Bibliography) to learn the histories of various immigrant groups; **Compare and contrast** the struggles, traditions, and dreams of the various groups past and present; **Fact find:** U.S. immigration laws past and present; contributions made to American society by immigrant groups; present-day immigrant groups; interview family members or community members to learn about their personal stories, ancestral or present; **Creative expression:** create a *collage* of information about present-day immigrants; *write* a poem, story, or essay about the person interviewed; or do a *photo collage* of person about his or her story; *make* a quote book to record inspiring words about *your* American Dream (American Dream Book); *write skits* about various immigrant groups; *plan and organize a Multicultural Celebration Day* and invite family and community members.

Materials: Copies of *Hope in New York City* and other fiction books about immigration (students read *Hope* and choose one other fiction book from the Bibliography); Internet access and/or library; Non-fiction books (see Bibliography); Construction paper and materials to make a quote book (American Dream Book); Nora, the protagonist in *Hope in New York City*, memorizes poetry and each chapter in the book begins with a quote; an American Dream Book is an inspirational hobby to boost the spirits of students; Art materials to create posters, pictures, crafts, etc. for a Multicultural Celebration Day.

LESSON PLAN ONE

Procedure: Begin the unit with reading *Hope in New York City*

1. Discuss why the protagonist and her family came to NYC (the first book, *The Irish Dresser: A Story of Hope during The Great Hunger* can be referred to; what are Nora's struggles, dreams, shortcomings? Discuss main plot.

2. Discuss what NYC is like in 1849—tenement buildings, streets, market; how does it differ from rural Ireland? What kind of work do the children do on the streets? What do they sell?

3. Who are the other immigrants in NYC during this time period? Do they get along? Do they clash?

4. What was the *Nativist Movement*? Discuss fear of foreigners (xenophobia) and compare and contrast this period with the present.

5. What was the *Astor Theater Riot*? What were the causes that led up to it? Discuss the difference between protest and riot.

6. Read passages aloud from various chapters and discuss:

   a) Chapter Three—*Helga's Bakery*, pg. 19. Ask students if they have felt uncomfortable in a public place; suggest that even if there are no ethnic differences, there is still the possibility of feeling awkward and uncomfortable as individuals. How does Nora feel? Does she find dignity? How do you find dignity?

   b) Chapter Five—*Nora Listens to Languages of the World*, pg. 37. How do immigrants learn English and keep their own language, their own traditions? What traditions do Nora and her family keep and are there any they don't keep? Ask students if they speak another language; if so, have them recite the Pledge of Allegiance in their language; if there is more than one represented, have students recite together; how does it sound?

   c) Chapter 9—*We Are All Seashells*, pg. 65. How are we the same no matter what country we come from; no matter how different we are from one another?

   d) Chapter 12—*Conversation with Walt Whitman*, pg. 86. Read Walt Whitman poem Nora memorized; discuss it; why does Nora challenge him?

   e) Chapter 15—*Nora Finds Her Dancing Feet*, pg. 101. Does Nora begin to feel America is home? Is it important for immigrants to have a place to celebrate their traditions? What does home mean to us?

Activities:

1. *Creating an American Dream Book:* The *American Dream* is the belief that if we work hard enough and are determined, we can become successful and have prosperous lives. All through our history, people have come to America for freedom and to live better lives. There are stories of immigrants who came to America with dreams and little else, but became successful in this country. These are the "rags to riches" stories. Who are some of these people in history? Does the *American Dream* mean acquiring money and material comforts? Is there still an *American Dream* today? What was Nora's *American Dream?* How does Sean's *American Dream* differ from Nora's? What is your *American Dream?*

2. Nora was inspired by poetry and each chapter begins with a quote that enlightens or inspires. What inspires you? Reading passages, quotes, poetry, and dreaming helps us to become inspired to live good lives.

3. Create your own American Dream Book to keep your dreams in, including poetry, quotes, and passages from books. Make the *American Dream* a place within you that aspires to a life of love and success.

LESSON PLAN TWO – WHO WERE THEY?

Procedure: Divide the class into five groups of four to six students; each group will research the history of one immigrant group (19th century to early 20th century) using fiction and non-fiction books (see Bibliography, Internet).

1. What country did group come from? Research general background of countries represented.

2. Why did the immigrants come here? Persecution? War? Famine?

3. What were the religious beliefs, cultural traditions; i.e., food, music, dance?

4. How were the immigrants treated in America? Were certain immigrant groups more acceptable than others?

5. What specific contributions did each group make to America?

6. Students look up immigration laws that affected the various immigration groups.

Activities:

1. Each member of the group can be assigned a specific fact or facts to research; after bringing their information to the group, the group can discuss it and write a skit together about an experience or experiences of the immigrant group; these will be performed on *Multicultural Celebration Day* at the end of the unit.

Lesson Plan Three – Who Are You & Who Are They Now?

Procedure: Students will interview people to learn of their immigrant experience; they can choose a family member, neighbor, community member, or a recent immigrant to this country; if they cannot find someone, they can find a recent article about an immigrant in the newspaper, on the Internet, etc.

1. Students will write an essay, poem, story; take photographs or draw a picture about what they learn of their ancestral background and/or what they learn of a community member's background; important to obtain permission to photograph and share information with public.

2. Students compare and contrast the experiences of what they learned of past immigrants with what they learn from their family members or recent immigrants.

3. Students learn of present-day immigration laws and how they affect immigrants of today.

4. A collage of their artwork to be presented on *Multicultural Celebration Day.*

Multicultural Celebration Day

1. Family and community members are invited to a day of celebrating the immigrant experience of the past and present.

2. Students will display their work—essays, poems, stories, photos, drawings of their interviews; American Dream Books; perform group skits, invite ethnic dancers to the event (or dance themselves).

3. Volunteers—ethnic food; ethnic dancers; ethnic clothing.

4. Local newspaper and/or television station contacted to do a write-up of the event.

GLOSSARY

Amadawn (Amadan). The fool of the fairies in Celtic myth; the touch of the amadawn could make one mad.

Astor House Hotel. Hotel built by John Jacob Astor, a German-born fur trader who amassed enormous fortune.

a storin. Irish term of endearment (dear one).

Astor Place Opera House Riot. Years of antagonism between the struggling classes erupted in 1848 when 8,000 Irish and American working class people disrupted a performance of the English actor William C. Macready, who was playing the same role as their favorite American actor, Edwin Forrest. The two actors had been rivals for years. After the riot, 22 people had died and 150 were wounded.

Barnum, Phineas T. Ex-newspaperman from Connecticut who became the proprietor of the American Museum, a major tourist attraction in the 19th century.

B'Hoys. Slang for group of rude multi-ethnic boys; mostly American-born Irish youth; wore greased hair and loud checkered clothing; frequented dance halls and taverns.

bootblack. Enterprising youths with shoeshine kits in 19th century.

Booth, Junius Brutus. Actor who performed Shakespeare at the Bowery Theater.

Bowery Theater. A working class theater in the Bowery of Five Points that offered Shakespeare, melodramas, English operas, Italian singers, and farces.

brilla-bralla. Irish term for childish nonsense and excessive embellishments.

Broadway Theater. Theater for the fashionable and upper classes on Broadway Avenue.

California Gold Rush. Gold found at John Sutter's saw-mill in Sacramento, CA, in 1848; thousands of people came to search for gold in 1849 and were called the "forty-niners."

camphor. A white transparent waxy crystalline solid with a strong, pungent, aromatic odor found in wood of the camphor laurel; used for medicinal purposes.

céilí. (pronounced KAY-lee) An Irish term for a social gathering or party; can mean specifically a dance with live music.

Chanfrau, Frank. An actor in 1848 who played "Mose," a popular character in plays performed in the Bowery; Mose was native born, a rowdy fire-laddie B'Hoy, brawler, and usually Irish-Catholic.

Cliffs of Moher. One of Ireland's most spectacular cliffs in County Clare; tremendous views on a clear day.

coffin ship. Crowded and unsanitary ships en route to North America from Famine Ireland were coined this because of the many Irish immigrants who perished on them.

corn girls. Young girls who peddled and sold freshly cooked ears of sweet corn; one of the best known street trades.

Cúchulainn. Great warrior and hero in Irish myth.

dandy. Any man who wore elegant fashions and was groomed meticulously; sometimes effeminate.

Diamond, John. Irish-American, born in 1823, known as the greatest jig dancer in Five Points, New York.

Famine (The Great Hunger). 1845-1850—one million Irish poor perished and over two million emigrated due to loss of potato crop, starvation, disease, and cruel British colonialism.

Five Points. Notorious neighborhood of 19th century New York City; inhabitants were mainly immigrants; immense poverty and crime; international interest in the lively music, dance, and saloon culture of the area.

Forrest, Edwin. American Shakespearean actor in 19th century New York; performed plays in the Bowery and was a rival of the English actor William C. Macready, which catapulted the city into a theater riot in 1849.

Godey's Lady's Book. Popular women's magazine begun in 1830 featuring color fashion plates and serial stories.

guttersnipe. Homeless child who roamed and slept in the streets.

Macready, William C. English actor who played Shakespeare, performing in England and America; the rivalry between the American Shakespearean actor Edwin Forrest and Macready catapulted the city into a major riot.

Queen Maeve. (Medb) The Queen of Connacht is a strong warrior character in the literary epic *Cattle Raid of Cooley*.

Master Juba. William Henry Lane, a famous African-American jig dancer who performed in Five Points and London; competed with famous American jig dancer John Diamond.

milliner. One who makes or sells women's hats.

nativist. American born; Nativist Movement and political party (Know-Nothings); anti-Catholic and anti-immigrant movement to restrict voting, education, and citizenship of immigrants.

newsie. Independent business kids who paid cash for newspapers and sold them on the street in the 19th century.

old clothes-man. A peddler who wore layers of used clothing and hats to sell on the street in 19th century.

pishoguery. Irish slang for foolish superstition.

planxty. Strange music said to come from the fairy world (Irish myth).

plebeians. Lowest class in Roman society; figuratively, meaning common people.

Printing House Square. On Park Row across from City Hall in New York, home to dailies, weeklies, and major newspapers, including the Associated Press.

Public School Society. Formerly Free School Society renamed Public School Society in 1826; various charity and Protestant churches organized system to educate the city's children and provide religious instruction; not favorable to Roman Catholic children.

Rynders, Isaiah. Tammany Hall politician, owner of Empire Club (for sporting men and prizefighters), gang leader, saloon owner; swayed immigrants for Democratic vote.

seanachie. Irish storytellers.

sidhe. Derived from Irish word for mound or hill; believed to be where the fairy people lived; fairy.

slumming parties. Foreigners and wealthy people visited Five Points with a police escort to gawk and marvel at the poverty and other vices.

Stewart Mansion. Alexander T.; Belfast immigrant who established department stores and became wealthy in the 19th century.

sweatshops. Tenement apartments became small factories for sewing clothing, making artificial flowers, rolling cigars.

tenement. Large building crowded with small apartments for working class and poor families.

Whitman, Walt. American poet (1819-1892) who wrote exuberantly about New York City.

Wordsworth, William. American poet (1807-1882).

xenophobia. Fear of foreigners.

SELECTED BIBLIOGRAPHY

Alger, Horatio, Jr. *Ragged Dick, Or, Street Life in New York with the Boot Blacks*. New York: Penguin Books USA, Inc., 1990.

Alvarez, Julia. *How Tia Lola Came to Stay*. New York: Dell Yearling Books, 2001.

Anbinder, Tyler. *Five Points: The 19th-century New York City Neighborhood that Invented Tap Dance, Stole Elections, and Became the World's Most Notorious Slum*. New York: The Free Press, 2001.

Bial, Raymond. *Tenement: Immigrant Life on the Lower East Side*. Boston: Houghton Mifflin Company, 2002.

Burns, Ric, and James Sanders with Lisa Ades. *New York: An Illustrated History*. New York: Alfred A. Knopf, 1999.

Cohen, Sheila. *Mai Ya's Long Journey*. Wisconsin: Wisconsin Historical Society Press, 2004.

De Capua, Sarah. *How People Immigrate*. New York: True Book Series, Scholastic, 2004.

Fennell, Haywood, Jr. *Coota and the Magic Quilt*. Boston: Tri-Ad Veterans League Publishing, 2004.

Freedman, Russell. *Immigrant Kids*. New York: Puffin Books, Penguin Books USA, Inc., 1980.

Hesse, Karen. *A Time of Angels*. New York: Hyperion Paperbacks for Children, 1997.

Neale, Cynthia. *The Irish Dresser: A Story of Hope during The Great Hunger (An Gorta Mor, 1845–1850)*. Shippensburg, Pennsylvania: White Mane Kids, 2004.

Riis, Jacob A. *How the Other Half Lives*. New York: Penguin Classics, Penguin Books USA, Inc., 1997.

Williams, Mary. *Brothers in Hope: The Story of the Lost Boys of Sudan*. New York: Lee and Low Books, 2005.

THE AUTHOR

Cynthia Neale at a book signing.

An American with Irish ancestry, CYNTHIA G. NEALE has long possessed a deep interest in the tragedies and triumphs of the Irish during the Famine. Ms. Neale has written a play on the Famine as well as several essays and stories as a freelance writer. She holds a B.A. in Writing and Literature from Vermont College, Union Institute. A native of Watkins Glen, New York, she now resides in New Hampshire and is involved in several community organizations. She enjoys traveling to Ireland to experience its beauty and haunting mystery first-hand. Visit the author's website at www.cynthianeale.com.

— ALSO BY THE AUTHOR—

THE IRISH DRESSER
A Story of Hope during The Great Hunger
(An Gorta Mor, 1845-1850)

The story of Nora McCabe and her family begins when Nora crawls into an old dresser that brings her from her parents' beloved Ireland to America to escape the Irish Famine. It is aboard the ship, inside the dresser, that Nora lives an adventure that transforms her life and turns hope into a reality.

ISBN 978-1-57249-344-5 · Softcover $7.95

— OF RELATED INTEREST —

THE WHISPERING ROD
A Tale of Old Massachusetts
Nancy Kelley

The story of Hannah Pryor brings to life the very different world of the Puritan Massachusetts Bay colony in the mid-17th century. Yet the dramatic story of Quaker preacher Mary Dyer reveals a fight for human rights and sheds light on the influence of women on American history.

ISBN 978-1-57249-248-6 · Hardcover $17.95

THE FORGOTTEN FLAG
Revolutionary Struggle in Connecticut
Frances Y. Evan

In 1964 a stained, old American flag is found in the attic rafters of a colonial farmhouse. The mystery of the flag's discovery is revealed as the story returns to the year 1779. *The Forgotten Flag* is the story of courage and sacrifice in a small community of ordinary townsfolk who make a stand against oppression and injustice.

ISBN 978-1-57249-338-4 · Softcover $5.95

WHITE MANE PUBLISHING CO., INC.

To Request a Catalog Please Write to:
WHITE MANE PUBLISHING COMPANY, INC.
P.O. Box 708 • Shippensburg, PA 17257
e-mail: marketing@whitemane.com

"Irish immigrant life in 1840s New York lives and breathes through these pages. Cynthia Neale's writing is vivid and lively—so much so that we forget we are reading history and, instead, just snuggle up for another well-told tale about Nora McCabe."

—Áine Greaney, Author of
The Sheepbreeders Dance
and *The Big House*

"...a story of triumph over adversity that teaches the importance of love, history, and unity."

—Haywood Fennell, Sr.,
Author/Playwright

Printed in the United States
201950BV00002B/1-165/P

9 781572 493872